MYSTIC CROSSROADS

Book Two of the Beyond the Crossroads Series
A Novella

Erica Fimbrez

Erica's Story House

Published by Erica's Story House

Print: ISBN: 979-8-9929578-4-6

eBook: ISBN: 979-8-9929578-5-3

Book Cover by Sienna Rose

First edition 2025

Printed in the United States of America

Contents

Chapter 1

Tom Jones

Red Earth 2020–Texas, Adams Correctional Institution for Women

Andrea Perez had been locked up for a little over one year, with twenty-four more still hanging over her head. At fifty-six years old, she was no longer the cunning beauty who once turned heads and manipulated lives, just another inmate with tired eyes and a slow gait. The days bled into each other, routine and regret wearing down whatever edges she had left.

She was sentenced to 25 years in prison after being convicted on multiple felony charges, including DUI-related offenses that resulted in the death of her daughter and the critical injury of her friend. She had fled the scene and was later linked to the assault of a responding officer during her attempted escape.

Three cells down from Andrea lived seventy-six-year-old Julia Costa, serving time for her role in the murder of her own son, Victor Costa, the man who fathered both of Andrea's children, David and Molly.

Julia lives in quiet misery now, a shell of the woman she once was. The realization that she can no longer bend people to her will has hollowed her out. Around here, no one fears her; most of the women are chasing power of their own.

Andrea too has been forced to accept the limits of her charm and cunning ways. The old tricks no longer work, not in a place full of hardened women who've seen it all. After more than a few humiliating fights, she's learned the unspoken rule: stay quiet, stay small, and try to disappear.

Julia often thought back to that day, just last year, the day they brought her in-chains to the Gilson Police Station. The air had tasted strange, metallic. And Andrea had just been arrested hours earlier, slumped in a holding chair with blood on her face and nothing left to bargain with.

They were summoned not out of sympathy, but because David Costa, Julia's grandson, Andrea's son, had vanished. Along with his three young daughters. And a man named Josh Coleman.

Chief Edmonds had walked into the room like a man who had just witnessed something the human brain wasn't built to process.

"There was a haze," one of the officers had said. "A blue mist. Moving like it was alive."

Andrea had sat silent, motionless. But Julia had seen it, the flicker of recognition in her eyes.

They'd asked their questions, filed their reports, and never brought it up again.

Now, one year later, Julia sat on the edge of her cot, head bowed, listening. Three cells down, Andrea was doing the same.

Two correctional officers strolled past the row of cells, voices drifting through the bars.

"Can't believe the Chief's really hanging it up," one said. "Thirty-two years. Crazy."

"After what he saw last year? I'm surprised he lasted this long," the other replied. "That whole haze thing? Visitors and an inmate vanishing into thin air?"

"Yup. Still creeps me out. You know the only thing they found after it happened?"

The first one paused. "What?"

"A mirror. Just lying there on the floor. Apparently one of the girls dropped it. It's still in the evidence locker. No one ever touched it."

Their footsteps faded into the corridor.

Julia raised her eyes slowly toward the bars.

Andrea hadn't moved, hadn't spoken.

But Andrea knew.

She heard it. Every word.

And for the first time in over a year, Andrea Perez was fully awake.

If that mirror was what she thought it was, she would have to find a way to get it.

What she didn't know was that, three cells down, Julia was thinking the same thing.

Julia's logic was simple: with David and the girls missing, and no one to claim their belongings, she considered herself next of kin. She didn't know if the small mirror left behind by David or one of the girls meant anything, but it didn't matter. She should have something of his. Why not?

After all, she was in here because she'd wanted to make sure he was never taken from her.

Not by Andrea.

Even if it meant hiring someone to kill them both, her own son and Andrea.

They were planning to take David from her.

But the gunman only found Victor.

And that was enough.

⸺◆⸺

Julia had put in a request to claim the mirror. She knew it was a long shot, they probably wouldn't allow her to have it in the facility, but she had to try.

Andrea had done the same.

The twin request triggered the warden to send a letter to Chief Edmonds of the Gilson Police Department.

Chief Edmonds, just three days away from retirement, sat at his desk. After reading the letter, he sat back on his chair, eyes narrowing.

Why would these two women request the mirror? What do they know about it?

The chief glanced at his cluttered desk, remembering that day David visiting Coleman. The three girls, the blue swirling smoke. The struggle, and they were gone. No signs of escape. No compromised exits. He remembered his officers, and himself, too paralyzed with fear to act.

Trying to write that report had been the hardest thing he'd done in his career. Hell, it was impossible. There was no acceptable explanation.

He picked up the phone and dialed the warden of Adams Correctional Institution for Women.

"Warden Harris? Hey Ronetta, it's Todd of The Gilson PD."

Warden Ronetta Harris, a poised African-American woman with a thick southern Texas drawl, answered smoothly. "Good afternoon, Chief Todd. You countin' down the days till retirement?

The Chief smiled, "Very much so. You still coming down to the station tomorrow for the party?"

"Todd, you know I'mma be there," she said, teasing. Then her tone shifted slightly. "I'm guessing you got the letter?"

"I did." He paused. "Ronetta, I'd like to come by and speak to both women. You know that case was never closed, and I'd like to ask them a few questions about their request, see what they really know. I'll be bringing my lead detective with me. Can you make that happen?"

"This afternoon works," she said. "But you'll need to be wrapped up by 4 p.m."

The chief looked at his watch. "We're on our way." He hung up, then immediately called his lead detective.

"Marquez? Drop whatever you're doing, we're heading to Adams. You're coming with me."

He opened his office door just in time to see Detective Marquez standing there, fist raised mid-knock.

"Marquez. Come in."

"What's going on at Adams?" Marquez asked, brow furrowed in confusion.

The Chief didn't sit. "Marquez, you were there that day," he said. "The day Coleman, Costa and the girls vanished."

Detective Marquez narrowed his eyes, tilting his head slightly. "Yeah, I remember."

Chief Edmonds nodded. "David Costa's grandmother, Julia Costa, and his mother Andrea Perez requested to claim the mirror. The one stored in the evidence room." Marquez frowned. "They have to know damn well they're not allowed to have a mirror inside the facility."

"Exactly," the Chief said, "So why ask for it unless they know something we don't?"

The detective watched as Chief Edmonds, pulled on his sweater and headed toward the door.

Without another word, Marquez followed, already falling into step behind him.

At Adams Correctional Institution for Women, Warden Harris had set Chief Edmonds and Detective Marquez up in a small interview room, concrete walls, fluorescent lights, and just enough space for uncomfortable truths.

"Just so you know," Warden Harris said, pausing at the door, "these two women hate each other. I wouldn't put them in the same room unless one of y'all wants to play ring referee."

She gave a hearty chuckle, then nodded toward the wall phone. "When you're ready, just pick up the line and let 'em know who to bring in."

With that, she shut the door behind her.

The Chief turned to Marquez. "Call for Andrea Perez first."

Marquez lifted the phone and spoke quietly to the officer on the other end. A few minutes later, Andrea was led into the room, wrists shackled, her expression unreadable.

Detective Marquez gestured to the metal chair across from them. "Have a seat, Andrea."

She sat slowly, eyes flicking between the two men. "Well," she said, "this feels familiar."

The chief introduced himself and Detective Marquez, then gave a slight nod to his partner to lead.

"Andrea, you submitted a request to claim property belonging to David Costa," Marquez began.

"Yes, I did. He's... he was my son. I should be able to make that claim."

Andrea realized she answered a little too quickly. And from the look in their eyes, she could tell they noticed. Suspicion hung in the silence.

Chief Edmonds parted his lips to speak but glanced at Marquez, then thought better of it... then closed them again.

Marquez kept his tone even. "Can you tell us why you only requested the mirror?"

Andrea narrowed her eyes, confused. "What else was there to claim? I heard it was just a mirror."

"There was also a child's purse. A few small plastic toys," he said, watching her closely.

Andrea flicked her gaze from him to the Chief but said nothing.

After a long pause, Marquez continued. "Julia Costa also submitted a request to claim the items. As next of kin."

Andrea's eyes widened. "Are you kidding? She can't claim next of kin, she had her own son killed."

Chief Edmonds let out a dry smirk. "And you didn't kill your daughter?"

The room went still.

Detective Marquez didn't wait for her response. "Julia wants the mirror too."

Andrea's composure cracked. "Why does she want the mirror?"

She regretted the question the moment it left her lips.

"Why do *you* want it?" Marquez asked.

Andrea, slipping into her usual charm tactics, replied, "Just to be fair, why don't we let her have the purse and the toys... and I'll take the mirror?"

Detective Marquez, recognizing Andrea had slipped into her old manipulation mode, kept his expression flat.

"Julia will want everything," he said. "Including the mirror."

He didn't know that for certain, but he wanted to see Andrea's reaction. And now he was sure of one thing: she wanted that mirror badly.

Andrea didn't respond.

Chief Edmonds glanced at his watch. 3:02 p.m. Fifty-eight minutes left.

He cleared his throat. "Okay. We'll talk with Julia and call you back once we've decided who'll receive the property."

Andrea met his gaze, holding it for just a moment before looking away.

Detective Marquez picked up the wall phone and requested the next interview.

A few minutes later, Julia Costa was brought into the room.

As the door shut behind her, Andrea was escorted back to the dayroom.

She scanned the space automatically and immediately noticed Tiny.

Tiny was a legend in Adams. Seventy years old, six-foot-two, easily two-hundred pounds. Still strong. Still dangerous. Still very much a bully.

And still obsessed with Tom Jones, the 1960s and '70s heartthrob singer whose hips and voice made half the world faint.

Everyone stayed clear of her. If you had to talk to Tiny, you agreed with everything. No exceptions.

She claimed Tom Jones was waiting for her "on the outs." She carried his photos like they were sacred, pressed to her chest or tucked in her waistband.

If those pictures went missing, even for a minute, someone got hurt.

And let's just say: it was never pretty.

One day, Julia and two other inmates made the mistake of laughing at Tiny.

"Tom Jones is not waiting for you now, and never has," one of them said with a snicker.

All three women ended up in the emergency room.

After Tiny, sometimes called Big Tiny, was released back into general population, no one dared mention Tom Jones again. Ever.

While Julia sat with Chief Edmonds and Detective Marquez, Andrea had an idea.

A terrible, perfect idea.

She needed to make sure Julia never got that mirror.

Across the dayroom, Andrea watched as Tiny shuffled away from her usual corner... carrying a few of her precious Tom Jones photos, not realizing that she'd left several behind, scattered on a chair

Unusual. Still, they were there.

Andrea knew the rhythm of the cameras. They panned from one side of the room to the other, always in slow, methodical arcs.

She waited... counted the beats... and when both lenses turned away, she moved. Just a few quick steps, one breath, and she snatched up the photos and tore them in half, clean, fast, quiet.

Then she turned to an inmate walking nearby and said under her breath, "You better steer clear of that table. I just saw Julia Costa rip Tiny's pictures before she got escorted out. If Tiny thinks you did it... well... I wouldn't risk it."

The woman's eyes widened. She bolted.

Andrea slipped away too.

Meanwhile, in the interview room, Detective Marquez picked up the phone.

"Send Andrea Perez back in," he said.

As Andrea was led in, Julia was being escorted out.

Back in the dayroom, Julia passed the table, unaware.

An inmate leaned toward Tiny, whispering in her ear.

Tiny looked down at the shredded remains of her Tom Jones photos. Then she looked up.

Her eyes locked on Julia. Fury radiated from her like heat off concrete.

And it was all aimed in one direction.

The Chief and Detective Marquez had seen enough in their interview with Julia. Her request for the items wasn't about sentiment. It was about control. Power. Dominance over Andrea. She hadn't shown any particular interest in the mirror itself. She just wanted everything... so Andrea would get nothing.

They released her.

Now Andrea sat across from them again, eyes shifting between the Chief and the Detective.

She noticed they hadn't shackled her this time, but she wasn't about to question a good thing.

By now, Chief Edmonds was certain: Andrea wanted that mirror. And she knew something, something she wasn't saying.

He didn't ease into it.

"I'm going to get to the point," he said, sharp. "Why do you want that mirror? And don't give me some bullshit about wanting a piece of your son."

Andrea held his gaze, but said nothing.

The Chief reached into his sweater pocket and pulled something out.

It was the mirror.

Andrea's eyes widened. Her eyes locked on the mirror.

"Chief?" Marquez's voice sharpened. "That's evidence. How the hell did you—?"

"I worked it out with the evidence tech," Edmonds interrupted. He knew damn well he shouldn't have it with him. But he also knew there was something about this mirror. Something that didn't belong in an evidence locker.

Marquez's eyes widened.

Then Andrea rose slowly, hand outstretched. "I'll take that."

Chief Edmonds let out a laugh, noticing the way her eyes locked on the mirror, hungry, almost feral. Like it was candy. Or fire.

And then she said it.

"I can help you find them. I know where they are. Josh, David, and the girls. Give me that mirror, and I'll show you."

Before he could respond, a loud siren blared through the facility.

Detective Marquez jumped from his chair. "I'm going to check it out," he said quickly.

The Chief nodded, never taking his eyes off Andrea.

As soon as Marquez left the room, Edmonds leaned forward.

"Show me how it works," he said quietly. "I'll find them."

Andrea let out a low laugh. "Believe me, Chief. If you don't let me help you, you'll regret it. I promise you this: you'll never find them without me."

Edmonds hesitated.

Then a knock at the door. Marquez's voice came through from the other side.

"It's a lockdown. This door's locked. I'll come back when it's over."

Andrea took the opportunity to grab the mirror from the Chiefs hand. But he had a stronger grip. As he pulled the mirror away from her, she was able to tap the mirror with her finger and slide it down. Then the blue haze began.

He shouted, "What did you do?"

Andrea smirked, "You wanted to know about the mirror? You wanted to know where they are? Well, in a few seconds... you'll get to find out."

Terrified, the Chief let go of his grip on the mirror and ran for the door... but it wouldn't budge. The facility was in full lockdown.

Detective Marquez could hear him shouting, screaming, "open the door!" But Marquez couldn't get it to open. Meanwhile the sirens wailed, and the blue haze inside the interview room thickened, swirling like a living thing. Andrea stood there smiling. The Chief couldn't escape it. The haze followed him to every corner. He ended up under the table. But it didn't matter, the vortex took him, along with Andrea.

Detective Marquez could only hear the sirens, no more shouting. No sounds, just silence. But when he looked down, he saw remnants of the blue, smoky haze. It was familiar.

When the sirens stopped, he could hear the sounds of door locks popping. He immediately opened the door, no chief, no Andrea and no mirror.

There were no windows, and he was outside of the only door to that little room. The impossible had happened again.

Still reeling, he made his way to the corrections station, where a small crowd had gathered.

"I'm Detective Marquez," he said. "What happened?"

One of the officers looked rattled. "There was a fight. Two old ladies (one of them, the one they call 'Big Tiny') just went berserk and killed the other."

Another officer added grimly, "The one who died... she's the same inmate I escorted into the interview room earlier." He paused. "Julia Costa."

Marquez stood frozen.

The Chief and Andrea were gone.

And Julia Costa was dead.

Chapter 2

The Arrival

Tanya flipped the sign on the door to Closed and slid the bolt into place. Outside, the afternoon light had dimmed just enough to blur the edges of the snow-covered sidewalk, casting a faint blue tint on the shop's windows. It wasn't late, but it had been quiet all day, and Tanya had plans.

Not dinner. Not rest.

Plans for the shop. Not something anyone would understand.

Plans she hadn't told anyone about.

She moved through the aisles, the soft creak of the floorboards following her as she turned off most of the overhead lights. Only the warm glow of the salt lamp behind the counter remained, casting soft amber light across the jars, crystals, and handwritten labels that filled the shelves.

It had been almost a year since the mirror vanished.

Most people had forgotten. Tanya hadn't She could still feel the space where it used to rest, a hollow in the air, like breath held too long.

She paused near the back wall and closed her eyes, just for a moment.

And that's when she felt it.

A low hum, deep in her bones. The air thickening. That shift in pressure that always came before...

A gust of cold wind swept through the shop, from nowhere, from everywhere. The salt lamp flickered.

And in the blink of an eye, the air rippled.

Then, suddenly, they were there.

Faces.

Eyes staring straight at her, wide, disoriented, and impossibly real.

Tanya blinked.

Then recognition struck.

Andrea. It was Andrea.

The man beside her wore a uniform, someone Tanya didn't recognize, but the woman...

She knew that face.

And it shouldn't have been there.

Tanya realized that somehow, someway, Andrea gotten a hold of the lost mirror. The one Josh and David lost when they made their escape from the Red Earth last year.

Tanya noticed the man in uniform looked disoriented, eyes wide, scanning the shop, then locking on her. He looked like he'd just stepped out of a dream.

"So, we meet again," Andrea said, a smirk playing across her lips.

Tanya squared her shoulders and lifted her chin. "Why are you here, Andrea? You don't belong here."

Andrea's smile widened: sharp, smug, dangerous.

Chief Todd Edmonds flinched at Tanya's words. He turned toward Andrea, his voice tight with confusion. "Where are we?"

"We're at Mystic Crossroads," Andrea answered, eyes never leaving Tanya. "Lincoln, Nebraska."

Tanya took a deliberate step forward, her gaze shifting to the Chief. "Who are you? And why are you here?"

Todd nodded politely. "Ma'am, I'm Chief Todd Edmonds, Gilson Police Department, Texas."

He glanced around the shop once more, then back to Tanya.

"I couldn't exactly tell you why I'm here," he added, turning toward Andrea, his brow tightening, "or how I got here."

"Oh, you're just plain Todd here," Andrea said, her voice smooth with mockery. "Where we are now, you're not a chief. Gilson, Texas doesn't even exist here."

Tanya said nothing. She was already thinking. Fast.

The man, Todd, didn't seem dangerous. Confused, maybe. Even polite. But Andrea?

Andrea was always dangerous.

Tanya considered calling the police, to report intruders in her shop. But she knew exactly what Andrea would do, she'd identify herself as Andri Perez, her Blue Earth counterpart. That would open a door Tanya didn't dare touch. It would drag Andri and her family into a mess they didn't deserve.

Before she could act, Andrea's voice broke into her thoughts.

"It was nice seeing you again," she said with a chuckle. "We really do have to go. But before we do, we'll need some cash. I know you have cash."

Tanya's eyes narrowed. "Andrea, I'm not giving you anything."

Andrea's smirk didn't falter.

In a flash, she reached over and yanked the service pistol from Todd's holster.

Todd shouted. "Hey! Give me that!"

Andrea stepped back quickly, creating distance, and raised the pistol, leveling it at both of them.

"Now, Todd," she said, her tone dripping with sarcasm. "If you want my help finding who we're here for, you're going to have to cooperate. Otherwise, you'll be stuck here. Forever. She'll probably have you arrested."

She glanced at Tanya, then back to him.

"This is a different world, Todd. A different Earth. You'll figure that out soon enough. You'll need me to navigate it."

She cocked her head, eyes daring him.

"So, are you coming with me or not?"

Todd looked at Andrea. Then at the gun. Then at Tanya.

After a tense beat, he said quietly, "Get the cash. Now."

Andrea smiled.

"Now we're talking."

Andrea turned to Tanya. "You heard him, get the cash."

Tanya stepped behind the counter. Andrea followed, hovering close.

That's when Tanya saw it, a glint of light as Andrea shifted.

Something metallic poking out of her front pocket.

Her breath caught.

The mirror.

Andrea had it.

And that was a very dangerous combination.

Tanya lowered herself to the drawer under the register, keeping her expression flat.

Her hand slipped past the cash and found her phone.

I can't call the police, she thought. *That'll make everything worse. But Josh... Josh will know what to do.*

With Andrea momentarily distracted, Tanya moved fast. She slid the phone behind a line of herb jars, screen angled out. A quick tap. Then another. She quietly opened the secure contact shortcut she had saved for Josh.

She didn't trigger the call yet, but when Andrea and Todd left, all it would take was a word.

She grabbed a small stack of bills, stood, and handed them over.

Andrea grinned, satisfied. But Tanya's mind was already moving ahead.

Todd rifled through the drawers behind the counter and came up with a roll of heavy-duty box tape, the kind used to seal shipping cartons.

Andrea snatched it from his hand. "This'll do."

Tanya didn't flinch as Andrea crouched down and began wrapping the tape tightly around her ankles, binding them to the legs of the wooden chair.

"Arms too," Andrea muttered.

Todd hesitated, but under Andrea's glare, he stepped forward and wound a strip around Tanya's wrists, pulling them behind the backrest and taping them together.

"Snug enough?" Andrea asked with a smirk, tearing the tape with her teeth.

Tanya said nothing.

She kept her gaze level, calm, but her thoughts were already with the phone behind the herb jars.

And Josh.

He'd come.

She just had to hold out long enough.

Andrea stood back, admiring her work as Tanya sat bound to the chair.

Then she straightened, pulled the pistol tighter into her grip, and said, "Now, where's your car?"

Tanya didn't answer right away.

Andrea's tone sharpened. "The keys. And where it's parked."

Tanya stared at her, silent.

Andrea stepped closer, lowering her voice. "If you lie to me, Tanya... we'll come back. And next time, we won't need tape."

Todd shifted uncomfortably nearby, but didn't say a word.

Tanya exhaled slowly. "It's around back. In the alley. Keys are in the drawer by the cash box."

Andrea tilted her head, assessing her.

"We'll see," she said, and gave Tanya one last smile.

Andrea and Todd found the minivan parked just where Tanya said it would be.

It was cold outside, and they both shivered as they got inside.

Andrea got into the driver's seat, started the engine, and turned on the heater.

Todd looked at her and said, "Damn woman, you've got a real darkness about you, that's for sure."

Andrea smirked, "Oh please. Like you're a saint. Give me a break."

"Where we going?" Todd asked.

"We're going to get us some hot food, warm clothes and coats and then I'm taking you to see Josh and David. Just as I promised."

Tanya could hear the sound of the minivan's engine fading into the cold Nebraska air.

She waited. Ten seconds. Twenty.

Just enough to be sure.

She inhaled through her nose, twisted her fingers inside the tape, and leaned her head toward the shelf behind her.

Voice low and steady, she whispered, "Call Josh."

A tiny chime answered. Then silence. Then ringing.

She closed her eyes.

"Come on, Josh. Pick up."

Josh was stirring a pot of chili on the stove when his phone lit up on the kitchen counter. He glanced at it, wiped his hands on a towel.

The screen read: Tanya.

His brow furrowed. He picked up. "Hey. Everything okay?"

There was a pause. Too long. Then Tanya's voice came through, flat and controlled.

"Andrea's back. She has the mirror. And she's looking for David."

Josh stood completely still.

The wooden spoon slipped from his hand, clattering against the edge of the pot.

Dinner was over.

Josh didn't respond right away.

He stared at the wall for a moment too long: processing, calculating, switching gears.

He grabbed his phone, pressed it tighter to his ear.

"Are you hurt?"

Tanya's voice was steady. "I'm fine. Tied up. Shaken. But fine."

"I'm on my way."

He hung up before she could answer, tossed the towel on the counter, and turned toward the hallway, only to find Shannon standing there.

She'd come out quietly, barefoot in jeans and a sweatshirt, her hair still damp from a shower. "I heard part of that," she said, voice tight. "What's going on?"

Josh crossed the room, already unlocking the cabinet near the back door. "Andrea's back," he said flatly. "She has the mirror. Tanya's okay for now, but she tied her up. She's looking for David."

Shannon went still, eyes sharpening.

Josh pulled out the old duffel, a flashlight, a burner phone, and his revolver. Before zipping it closed, he looked at her.

"The long gun's by the door," he said. "You know how to use it. And you know what to do."

Shannon nodded without hesitation. "Got it."

"Stay here. If anything feels off, anything, you call David, and lock this place down."

"Be careful, Josh."

He paused at the door. Just for a second. "I will."

Then he was gone.

Shannon stood in the quiet that followed, the click of the door echoing through the hallway. She walked to the front window and checked the street, just to be sure, then turned back toward the kitchen.

It still felt a little surreal sometimes, living here with Josh, in his quiet, fortress-like home just outside Ridgefield. A far cry from her old apartment in Lincoln, those incense-filled days behind the counter at Mystic Crossroads, when she'd worked side by side with Tanya and life was a little less complicated.

They'd grown close after Josh's last relationship ended. It hadn't been planned; nothing about them ever was, but somehow, piece by piece, it had turned into something real. And now? *Now* she was here. Watching over his home. Trusted and loved.

She walked calmly to the coat closet and pulled the rifle from behind the hanging jackets, then locked the front door and turned off the porch light.

"You know what to do," he'd said.

And she did.

Meanwhile, Josh made it to Mystic Crossroads in record time. He noticed the back door slightly ajar and rushed inside, his steps quick and urgent.

"Tanya!" he called out.

"Back here, behind the counter," she answered.

As he approached, she added, "Andrea was here with a middle-aged man. He said his name was Chief Todd Edmonds, from Gilson, Texas."

Josh stood still for a moment, the weight of Tanya's words sinking in.

Chief Todd Edmonds, from Gilson, Texas.

That meant Andrea hadn't just escaped. She'd brought someone with her. Someone who had no idea what world he was in.

He exhaled slowly. "I've got to call David."

Tanya, still rubbing her wrists, looked up. "You think she's really going after him?"

Josh didn't answer. He already knew.

He pulled out his phone and stepped toward the front of the shop, turning away as he hit the contact and raised it to his ear. It rang twice.

David picked up. "Hey. What's going on?"

Josh's voice was low, urgent. "It's her. She's back. And she's not alone."

A pause. "Andrea?"

"She's got the mirror, and she's looking for you."

Another silence.

Josh continued. "Get this. She brought someone from the other side... Chief Edmonds. Tanya's okay, but they tied her up, took her van, and now they're on the move. You need to get the girls and go."

David didn't hesitate. "Where should I take them?"

"I'll call you back once I know where she's headed. But go now. Don't wait."

"Copy that," David said. "And Josh, thanks."

Josh ended the call and looked back at Tanya, his expression shifting, like something had just clicked into place.

"I just thought of something," he said quietly. "If Andrea's after David..."

He paused. The words hung heavy.

"...then Chief Edmonds is after me."

After finding warm coats at the local Walmart, they grabbed food from the McDonald's inside and ate quickly by the front windows, barely speaking. They were in a hurry, and it showed.

Todd glanced around to make sure he wasn't overheard. "You say we have a couple of hours or so to get there. Then we have to ditch the minivan. Law enforcement might be out looking for us as we speak."

Andrea scanned the parking lot, then leaned in. "Well, I still have your gun. We could jack someone outside and—"

"No," Todd cut her off. "Carjacking someone's a great way to bring every cop in the state down on us. And hand over the gun. I'm pretty sure I'm the better shot."

Andrea's eyes narrowed. "Then what's your genius plan for getting another car?"

Todd crumpled his napkin, stood up, and said, "I've got a plan. Give me some cash. I need to pick up a few things."

Andrea handed him a handful of bills without asking questions.

Fifteen minutes later, they were walking the edge of the parking lot, quiet and deliberate. Todd spotted what he needed, an older sedan parked near the employee side entrance. He slipped in like he'd done it a hundred times.

A moment later, the engine coughed to life.

Andrea slid into the passenger seat, glancing back at the minivan now abandoned with the keys left in plain sight.

"Well," she muttered, "for an old man, you still got it."

Todd didn't look at her. "That was never in question."

And with that, they pulled out of the lot, just another car disappearing into the night.

"Todd, I'm impressed. You have skills. My hero," Andrea said in a flirty tone. She continued, "Tell me, what other skills do you possess?"

Todd rolled his eyes. "Don't even think about it."

Andrea blinked, surprised. "That's insulting."

Todd shot back, sharp and dry, "Andrea, I understand you were something a few years back, but there is no way I would ever think about hooking up with you in that way."

Andrea, insulted, snapped, "Oh, like you're Prince Charming, with women falling at your feet."

Todd smirked. "You just tried to."

She exhaled hard and muttered, "Whatever. Make a left onto the highway and keep going for about an hour and forty-five minutes."

"Wow. That long in this car with you? It's gonna seem longer," Todd said, turning onto the ramp.

They were quiet for a few minutes, the stolen car humming down the road as wide Nebraska fields stretched endlessly on both sides.

Then Andrea straightened in her seat, her eyes narrowing. "Wait a second."

Todd glanced over. "Now what?"

"Why are we driving all the way to Ridgefield?" she said, already digging into her coat pocket. "I've got the mirror. I can open a portal right now and take us straight to Ridgefield, straight to Andri's house."

Todd's brows drew together. "You want to open a portal from inside a stolen car?"

"I want to stop wasting time," she said. "We pull off into a field, somewhere no one's watching, I do the thing, and we're there. Easy."

He shook his head. "That's your solution? Magic mirror on the side of a cornfield?"

Andrea smiled. "Better than being stuck in this car with you for another hour."

"Pull off at the next lonely country road you see," Andrea said.

Todd didn't argue. He exited the highway and followed a winding rural road, then turned right onto an even narrower one. It was dark and empty, fields stretching out on both sides. He pulled to the shoulder, cut the engine, and turned off the headlights.

"Now what?" he asked.

Andrea pulled out the mirror, gently stroking its frame with her fingers. A slow smile crept across her face. "Now... we make our appearance at Andri's house."

Todd narrowed his eyes. "What, we just show up? No car? That doesn't seem like the smartest move."

Andrea didn't answer at first. She continued tracing slow circles on the back of the mirror, almost like she was listening to it.

Finally, she said, "We might not have a choice. But I want to try something. It may work."

"Wait." Todd held up a hand. "Before you do anything, what's the plan? We show up and then what?"

"You go up to the house," Andrea said. "Say you're an old teacher of Josh's. Ask if they know where to find him."

Todd turned toward her. "And then what?"

Andrea pulled the gun from her coat pocket and handed it to him. "I'm pretty sure that piece in your hand will do more than start a conversation. Whoever answers the door, Josh or not, they'll help us find David."

"You said you wanted to try something. What are you gonna do?" Todd asked.

"I'm going to concentrate on us making us appear in Ridgefield, down the street from Andri's house. Somewhere dark. And in this car." She looked hopeful. "If it works, the car comes with us."

She closed her eyes and exhaled slowly, focusing.

Todd watched her warily. "Andrea, I thought I had a messed-up mind. Yours works in the darkest, most twisted ways."

Andrea ignored him. She tapped the mirror and slowly slid her finger down its back.

A faint red haze flickered across the glass. Her eyes flew open. "No."

It was going to take them to the Red Earth.

At that exact moment, Todd's gaze shifted; he noticed flashing lights filling the rearview mirror. A patrol car was pulling up behind them. His heart spiked.

Shit.

He didn't want to break Andrea's concentration. He stayed frozen, sweat trickling down his temple.

The officer got out of the car and approached the driver's side window.

Andrea, oblivious, kept her eyes closed, muttering under her breath as she focused harder. She peeked, no more red haze, just a strange distortion in the air ahead. And then—

BUMP.

She jolted in her seat. A split-second bounce. She opened her eyes.

Still in the car.

Andri's house was just up ahead.

She turned to Todd, who sat frozen, hands gripping the steering wheel so tightly his knuckles had gone white.

Andrea grinned. "I did it. Car and all. So what's the matter with you?"

Todd didn't speak. He slowly turned his head and motioned toward the window.

Andrea followed his gesture.

And saw a pair of hands gripping the edge of the partially rolled-down glass.

Chapter 3

A Mirror and Plans

Ridgefield, Nebraska

The hands gripped the window.

Andrea's smile faded.

"What the hell is this? What did you do?"

Todd stayed frozen, foot pressing hard on the brake. "What do you mean, what did *I* do?"

Andrea scanned the area. Coyotes howled in the distance as she pushed open her door and stepped out.

"What are you doing?" Todd hissed, lowering his voice.

"We have to do something with him. We can't just leave—"

She stopped mid-sentence.

Frozen.

"Dammit, Andrea, what's wrong?" Todd asked, frustrated.

Andrea slowly turned toward him, her expression shifting.

"Ah... nothing, actually. We're good."

She smiled, then gestured toward the driver's side window. "Take a look."

Todd leaned over the edge, and recoiled.

Two hands still clutched the window frame.

Bloody. Detached.

No body in sight.

His stomach turned. He shoved the door open, scrambled out of the car, and threw up in the dirt.

"Oh, come on," Andrea said flatly. "Don't be such a wuss."

She leaned into the back seat, pulled out a plastic grocery bag, and started walking calmly toward the driver's side. "I'll toss the hands in this and dump them in that garbage can across the street."

Todd was still gagging. "What about the blood?"

Andrea crouched beside the door, scooping up snow in her bare hand. "We'll just wipe it off with this. Most of it'll hit the ground. Simple."

Todd stared at her, disturbed.

For the first time, she genuinely scared him.

"Todd, go to that house. Do as we planned. Make sure you have the gun. Bring whoever's unlucky enough to answer the door back to the car," Andrea ordered.

"Now?" Todd asked, still reeling from her behavior.

"Before it gets too late. If we wait, they'll grow suspicious and cautious."

Damn, Todd thought, watching her.

This woman is calculating. Dangerous. What the hell did I get myself into?

Andrea, puzzled, watched as Todd slipped back into the car, through the passenger door.

She walked over to him. "Todd? What are you doing? Go."

Todd didn't move. His jaw clenched as he slowly turned to look up at her. Andrea flinched, just slightly.

"I don't appreciate you barking orders and making demands," he said, his voice low and steady. "You're just an old, evil, calculating bitch, Andrea. And I'm really starting to hate this little game of yours."

Andrea turned away, gazing out at the dark fields. Her voice was eerily calm. "Fine, Todd. Then tell me, how do you expect to nab Josh and David, bring them back to face charges, without me?"

He hesitated. He did want to bring David in. But more than anything, he wanted Josh, wanted to wipe that smug look off his face and get the satisfaction of dragging him in himself.

"Okay," Todd muttered. "But no more barking orders. And for God's sake, curb that evil shit."

Andrea smirked. "Well, I just had another thought."

Todd groaned. "Oh no. What now?"

"You made a good point. I am older. But you're only a few years behind me."

"What's your point?" he asked, suspicious.

"My point is... we only have one gun. If they have a weapon, we're screwed. Molly could take me down without breaking a nail, and Josh and David? They'd fold you like laundry."

Todd furrowed his brow.

"Don't pretend it's not true," Andrea said, still facing forward, eyes narrowing. "They're younger. Stronger. Smarter in some ways. We need another plan."

Todd didn't like that look on her face, the one that meant she was already spinning the web.

Before he could speak, she added, "I have an idea. And don't worry..."

She turned to him and smiled.

"...I think you'll like it."

Todd rolled his eyes and muttered, "Fuck."

He turned to Andrea as she pulled the mirror from her coat.

This time, he didn't say a word.

She closed her eyes and concentrated.

A strange sensation rippled through him.

The air shimmered, distorted, just for a second, then snapped back to normal.

He opened his mouth to say something, but stopped.

Something felt... off.

He turned to Andrea.

There she sat; beautiful, radiant. Her dark hair was thick and glossy, her face smooth and flawless, lips full, eyes sparkling. And the grin on her face, wide, wicked, proud.

"Andrea?" he asked, confused.

"Todd," she cooed, raising her eyebrows flirtatiously.

"Wow. You are handsome. How does it feel to be twenty-five again?"

She laughed, low, dark, delighted.

He blinked and turned toward the rearview mirror.

There it was.

His face. Young. Strong jawline. Bright eyes. No gray. No lines.

His hands ran down his chest and arms.

His muscles felt solid again. Alive.

He smiled. "Damn..."

"I told you you'd like it," Andrea said, leaning back with satisfaction. "I am unstoppable with this mirror."

His smile slowly faded.

More like dangerously unstoppable, he thought.

Andrea turned to him, eyes trailing slowly down his frame.

"Now we have a chance to kick some ass," she said, her tone low and sultry.

"But I think we should train first... you know, work out a little."

She smirked. "Besides, it's too late to storm them tonight. We'll go back tomorrow."

Todd wanted to protest. Wanted to shut it down.

But when he opened his mouth, her eyes locked onto his, and he hesitated.

What the hell...

It had been a long time.

And she did look good.

He was surprised at what he was thinking. He knew he'd probably regret it in the morning.

They drove to the next town, quiet the whole way.

And got a room.

Together.

Andri Perez was washing dinner dishes when she noticed headlights pulling into the circular driveway.

It was dark outside, but she recognized the car, it was David, and the girls.

Surprised to see them on a weekday night, especially after dinner, she dried her hands and walked to the side door to greet them.

Fourteen-year-old Paula came in first, followed by the twelve-year-old twins, Daphne and Delilah, all carrying overnight bags and sleeping bags. David followed close behind.

Andri immediately caught the tension in his face.

"What's going on?"

"Mom, we're staying here tonight," David said, setting down a duffel bag.

"Of course, but... why? What's going on?" she asked, growing uneasy.

David watched as the girls headed downstairs toward the basement. Then he looked back at her.

"Andrea's back."

Andri's eyes widened. "What? How?"

"Josh says she showed up at Mystic Crossroads, with that police chief, the one Josh and I escaped from. According to Tanya, Andrea has the mirror. They tied her up."

Andri gasped.

"Josh is with her now. She's safe," David continued. "But Andrea knows this house, Mom. If she's coming for me; this is where she'll show up. Josh thinks they're probably already on their way."

"Where's Drew?" David asked.

"He's in the bedroom watching the game," Andri said, already moving. "I'll go get him."

David stepped into the living room and spotted Nora in her rocking chair, watching TV. He walked over and gently placed an arm around her shoulders.

"Hi, Grandma."

Nora smiled and reached a hand up to his cheek, drawing him in for a soft kiss. He smiled.

A moment later, Drew stepped out of the bedroom, his dark hair tousled, streaked with gray, wearing sweatpants, a T-shirt, and slippers.

"She's on her way here?" he asked. Straight to the point.

"I think so," David said. "And we shouldn't underestimate her. She's dangerous."

Drew nodded, then turned to Andri. "Check the basement windows. Make sure they're locked."

David readied his pistol. Drew reached for his rifle. Both men moved with a quiet urgency, lowering lights, checking locks, securing the perimeter.

Then Nora spoke.

"Leanne."

They both turned. Nora hadn't spoken very much since her diagnosis of Alzheimer's four years earlier, and the sound of her voice, clear, deliberate, stopped them in their tracks.

"What about Leanne, Grandma?" David asked.

Nora repeated, voice softer but insistent. "Leanne."

Drew looked at her, then at David. "Don't worry. I don't think Andrea knows where Leanne lives. Besides... she's after you. Not Leanne."

It was nearing 10:00 p.m. when Drew sent everyone to bed. He and David agreed to take shifts, keeping watch through the night and monitoring the Ring camera for any sign of Andrea.

But the night passed quietly.

No headlights.

No shadows.

No Andrea.

Only the weight of waiting.

The next morning, David sat at the dining room table, working on his laptop. Though the house was calm, his eyes still flicked toward the window every few minutes, still on alert.

They had already called the school, reporting that the girls and Lanix were out sick with the flu. It was easier than trying to explain the truth.

That morning, Molly returned home. She'd just finished moving out of her apartment and was back under her mothers' roof, for now. In three weeks, she'd be leaving for boot camp. She had enlisted in the Army.

In the kitchen, Andri and Drew sat at the table, drinking coffee and talking quietly when Molly walked in.

"Okay, what's going on?" Molly asked, already sensing something was off.

David told her everything.

"And she's coming here?" she asked.

"I think so," David said.

Just then, Nora walked into the kitchen.

Molly walked up and gave her a hug.

Andri stood from her chair. "Mom, I have your breakfast ready."

Nora sat at the table and began eating, then paused as her expression darkened.

"Leanne," she said, frowning.

Everyone exchanged glances.

"Mom, what about Leanne?" Andri asked, approaching her.

Nora looked up, eyes intense, almost frightening.

"Help her," she said.

Then she turned to Andri. "Mija, she needs help."

Just then, Lanix and the girls walked into the kitchen for breakfast. Lanix had overheard.

"Molly, take me there. I want to help Aunt Leanne."

Molly didn't hesitate; she grabbed her keys and headed for the door.

David called out, "Molly, wait. I'll call Josh, he lives just down the street from her."

"I'm still going," Molly replied.

Drew added quickly, "David, if Molly's going, you should go with her. We'll stay here and watch the kids."

"I'm going too!" Lanix insisted.

"Lanix," Andri said gently, "I know you want to help your Aunt Leanne. But you're supposed to be out sick today, you can't go anywhere. Between Josh, David, and Molly, Leanne will be fine."

Lanix stamped his foot, frustrated.

Drew stepped in. "Lanix... your time is coming. Before long, you'll be old enough to help protect this family. I'll talk to Josh, together, we'll get you trained for that role. Would you like that?"

Lanix's eyes lit up. "Yes."

Drew nodded. "Good. Now go ahead and eat your breakfast."

David and Molly rushed out the door.

Andri picked up her phone and called Josh.

Not far from the hotel, Todd had already dumped the stolen car and found another one.

As they drove, the early morning light spilled across the sky, soft shades of blue stretching wide over the horizon. Todd glanced up through the windshield, eyes squinting at the brightness.

It hit him; he could see the color. Sharper. Cleaner. The way he used to.

His youthful eyes adjusted quickly, no blurring, no ache.

The sky was a vibrant blue. So alive.

He shook his head, still trying to wrap his mind around it.

Being twenty-five again wasn't just a mirror trick, it was real. It felt real in his bones.

But before he could dwell too long, Andrea's voice cut through the silence.

She leaned forward, eyes locking on a pair of figures exiting a house up ahead.

"That's David and Molly," she said, grinning.

"Follow them."

———◇———

Tanya sat in her home office; papers spread across the desk, future plans for Mystic Crossroads.

They had appeared mysteriously just the day before, but she hadn't had a chance to review them, not with Andrea's unexpected arrival throwing everything into chaos.

Still, as she looked them over now, Tanya knew exactly where they came from.

Anio.

She slowly unrolled the top sheet, fingers brushing across the paper like it might whisper to her. There were sketches. Symbols. Markings she didn't fully understand, but felt deep in her bones. They weren't ordinary architectural plans. They were layered. Alive.

Guidance, she thought. Instructions.

Anio wasn't just showing her where to expand the shop.

He was preparing her for something more.

Tanya leaned forward, eyes narrowing. A line near the bottom caught her attention, one written in a language she only recognized in dreams.

She exhaled softly and whispered, "Okay, Anio... I'm listening."

As she turned to the second page, the design shifted. It wasn't just floorplans anymore. It was a map. A topographic grid etched with energy lines, intersecting at powerful nodes.

Sedona.

Her breath caught. The plans outlined a new structure, a relocation of Mystic Crossroads, built around what Anio had labeled as active convergence points.

Gateways.

Portals.

Tanya's fingers trembled slightly as she traced the lines. Fortified borders... layered protection glyphs... and, at each key point, names.

She blinked.

Andrea (Andri) Perez.

Leanne Perez.

Joseph (Joe) Perez.

Michael Perez.

Nora's children

The Perez family were marked as the guardians.

Tanya sat back, stunned.

Why them?

And what would happen to the portal here in Nebraska?

She looked over at the familiar Mystic Crossroads layout on her wall, then down at the glowing plans in front of her.

She stared at the names on the page a moment longer.

Nora's children.

Then she looked down, her hands resting gently on the paper.

Anio... she asked silently, what happens to the shop here in Lincoln?

Does it get sold? Am I moving to Sedona?

And the portal, this portal, what becomes of it?

Her heart ached just asking the questions.

Mystic Crossroads wasn't just a shop. It was her sanctuary. Her calling. Her life.

She closed her eyes for a moment, waiting, not for a voice, but for a feeling.

A pull. A whisper in the current.

She stared at the sketch, the glyphs glowing faintly under her fingertips.

So... the portal here in Lincoln would close.

Mystic Crossroads here in Lincoln will be no more.

And she... wasn't moving to Sedona.

Her heart tightened. The ache wasn't just emotional; it was cellular. As if her body already knew what her mind was only now beginning to accept.

She looked down again, tears pricking the corners of her eyes.

If not Sedona... then where, Anio?

Where am I going?

What will I be doing?

A hush settled over the room.

Then, soft, like wind brushing the veil between worlds, she felt it.

You are not moving... the message came, not in words, but in something deeper. *You are transitioning.*

To where? she asked, her breath held.

The answer came not as a place, but a truth.

To us.

A merging. A returning.

Not an end, but a reunion.

She would become part of the force that had guided her for so long.

Part of the energy that guarded the portals... that watched over the others...

That whispered to the living from just beyond.

Her time here was coming to a close.

Not today. Not tomorrow. But soon.

And when it came... she wouldn't be afraid.

She turned the next page.

More diagrams. Architectural layouts. But this time, her eyes caught a handwritten note, neat, elegant script that hadn't been there a moment before.

"Take these to Joe Perez. Meet him in Sedona. I will arrange everything."

Her brow furrowed. Sedona? Now?

Before she could question it, a second message began to form, ink blooming across the page like breath against glass.

"Transport will be provided. Timing is in my hands."

She exhaled slowly, absorbing the gravity of it.

People would come. Builders. Protectors. Land stewards.

The pieces would move into place, not by chance, but through Anio's unseen orchestration.

Everything would happen... in his time.

Still, a flicker of practicality surfaced.

What about the money? The permits? The logistics...?

But even before she could finish the thought, a soft warmth swept through her chest, as if answering her doubt before she finished forming it.

"All is taken care of."

The message was final. Quiet, but resolute.

Just then, Shade, her sleek black cat, rubbed against her legs, purring softly.

Tanya looked down and smiled. "Should I bring Shade with me?" she asked aloud, speaking to the air but truly to Anio.

The answer didn't come in words.

It vibrated through the walls of her office: low, resonant, undeniable.

"No."

Tanya froze. Shade paused, her piercing, light blue eyes lifting to meet hers.

Then, quieter, but just as clear, came the second part of the message:

"Shade has another mission."

Tanya blinked, her brow furrowed. She looked at the cat, then back toward the space where Anio's message lingered.

Mission? Shade? she thought, stunned.

The cat flicked her tail and trotted off, as if she already knew.

Tanya wasn't sure whether to laugh or be unnerved.

She took one last walk through Mystic Crossroads, each step echoing with memory.

She wouldn't be coming back, and somehow, the place already knew it too.

Chapter 4

Eerie Illusions

After Josh got the call from Andri, he sprinted to Leanne's house, just down the street.

Her car was still in the driveway. She was home.

He grabbed the front doorknob. Locked.

Fumbling with his key, he shoved it into the lock and turned. Nothing. He tried again. Still nothing.

"Mom!" he shouted, pounding on the door. No answer.

He ran around to the back and tried the rear door. Also locked. He checked the windows, sealed.

Her car was here. She had to be inside.

"Mom!" he yelled again, voice rising.

No response.

Without hesitating, he grabbed a garden stone and smashed the side window. Glass scattered. He reached in, unlocked the door, and burst inside.

As soon as he was inside, Josh stopped cold.

Silence.

Not the kind you get when no one's home. This was thick, unnatural. Like the air had been vacuumed out of the house.

His eyes swept the room, and then locked onto her.

Leanne.

Sitting on the couch.

Perfectly still.

Only the back of her head visible.

"Mom?" he called out, voice tight.

No reply.

He stepped forward slowly. The wooden floor creaked beneath his feet.

Rounding the couch, he stopped again.

Her hair hung over her face, stringy, unmoving. She was slightly rocking back and forth, back and forth, like something out of an old nursery rhyme gone wrong.

"Mom...?" he whispered.

No answer.

He leaned in, heart racing, and gently reached out to move her hair from her face.

What he saw made his blood run cold.

Her head snapped toward him, unnaturally fast.

Her face was contorted into a wide, stretched smile that looked carved into her skin.

And her eyes...

Solid black.

No whites. No pupils. Just void.

And at the center of each...

A thin red circle, like a glowing bullseye.

They started to spin.

Faster.

And faster.

And faster.

Josh stumbled backward, frozen in horror.

The red circles pulsed, then exploded, shooting out beams of searing crimson like sharpened light.

He dove to the floor, just in time.

The beams sliced overhead, burning into the wall behind him with a hiss.

He crawled behind the couch, breath heaving, eyes wide with terror.

From above him came laughter, but it wasn't his mother's voice.

It was warped. High-pitched.

Playful and cruel.

Like something that enjoyed controlling her.

Josh's throat tightened.

He couldn't leave. He couldn't just leave her like this.

He pressed himself against the back of the couch, trembling.

And then—BANG!

The front door burst open. David and Molly flew through it.

Molly screamed as her leg slammed into a table and she collapsed in pain.

David landed in a crouch right beside Josh.

Before either of them could speak—

SLAM!

The door snapped shut behind them like it had a will of its own.

And from the living room...

Leanne's laughter rose again.

Only now. It wasn't just laughter.

It was welcoming.

David, noticing Josh had gone pale, grabbed his shoulder and whispered, "What the hell is going on?"

Before Josh could answer, they both looked up.

And there she was.

Leanne's face, distorted, unnatural, was peering over the edge of the couch.

Her body hadn't moved. Still seated, still facing forward.

But her head had twisted completely around.

That same wide, terrifying smile stretched across her face like her skin was barely holding it together.

Josh's breath caught.

Her eyes, still pitch black, now glowed faintly.

And in the center...

The red circles had started spinning again.

He didn't wait.

"We have to run," Josh said, voice sharp, eyes locked on hers. "Now."

Just as they got up to run, Leanne laughed, a high, broken sound that crackled through the air.

The lights flickered.

Molly let out a low scream as her injured leg buckled. Josh and David rushed to help her, trying to get her upright and moving toward the door.

The lights flickered again, longer this time, casting shadows that didn't match their movements.

Josh looked back.

Leanne was standing now.

Closer than before.

Still smiling.

But her face, her skin, looked wrong. Waxen. Stretched. Not human.

That wasn't his mother.

The lights flickered again.

When they blinked back on, she was gone.

Josh spun in a circle, heart racing. "Where is she—?"

Before he could finish, he heard David shout:

"Molly!"

She was gone too.

Both men shouted her name.

A soft whimper answered.

They turned, eyes locking on the dining room.

And what they saw nearly stopped their hearts.

Molly sat stiffly at the dining table, dressed like an old-fashioned porcelain doll.

Her cheeks were painted in perfect, exaggerated red circles.

Her lips a bright, eerie pink. Her eyes, still Molly's eyes, were wide with terror, silently begging for help.

In front of her: tiny, delicate teacups arranged neatly on lace-trimmed saucers. Doll-sized.

And beside her...

Leanne.

Hair curled in stiff ringlets. Face powdered white.

Her lips were painted in a tiny, puckered rosebud shape, doll-like and unsettling, as if smiling and frowning all at once.

Her teeth, when she smiled, were stained a ghastly yellow, jarring against the pale makeup and prim lipstick, like rot beneath porcelain.

Her dress was lace-trimmed and high-collared, like something pulled from a haunted attic.

She held a tiny porcelain teapot and poured pretend tea with slow, deliberate motion.

Then, smiling wide, she looked up at Josh and David.

Her eyes sparkled with something cold. Ancient. Wrong.

She gestured toward two empty chairs at the table.

Two more tea settings waited.

Suddenly, everything changed.

Josh blinked.

He wasn't in the dining room anymore.

He was standing upright, stiff, in the middle of a ballroom.

A grand one.

Faded chandeliers dripped from the ceiling. The walls were papered in dusty gold and peeling crimson.

The air was heavy, perfumed with roses and rot.

A soft waltz played from nowhere.

The string instruments were slightly off-key.

He looked down.

He was dressed in formal evening attire, not a modern tuxedo, but something older. Tailored and crisp, with the elegance of the Regency era.

He reached for the tie at his neck, but his hands... they wouldn't move freely.

He was holding someone's hand.

Across from him, a woman in a ball gown, spinning slowly in time with the music.

Her dress, once white, now yellowed and frayed. Her long gloves stained.

And then she looked up.

It was Shannon.

At least it had been.

Her once-soft features now sagged and sunken, her eyes glazed over with the pale film of death.

Her cheeks had begun to rot away. One eye socket leaking slow, pale maggots.

And her mouth—

Her rotting lips parted.

She leaned in.

Her voice came in a raspy whisper, teeth black and crooked beneath flaking lipstick:

"Kiss me, Josh."

Josh gasped, but he couldn't let go.

His body wouldn't move.

His feet stepped in rhythm.

His arms followed hers.

He was dancing with the corpse of someone he loved.

He spotted a Bald Man, his skin eerily smooth, not rotting, playing the violin out of tune.

The notes screeched. He laughed… mocking.

Watching.

His eyes darted across the ballroom, searching for David. For Molly. For anyone.

But David was already gone.

David blinked.

He was no longer in the house. No more walls. No furniture. No lights.

Just gray.

A sky the color of ash loomed overhead, heavy and unmoving. The air smelled of iron and dust.

He was standing on a makeshift wooden platform, high above a silent crowd.

His hands were bound.

A rope dangled from above.

He looked down.

The crowd was staring up at him.

But not strangers.

Andrea. Smirking in a blood-red dress.

Kathy, his ex-wife, arms crossed.

Ruben, his ex-best friend who'd stolen Kathy from him, standing beside her with that same smug tilt of the head.

And then Julia Costa. His grandmother.

Still wearing the uniform from the prison infirmary.

Eyes hollow. "I did it for you. Don't you understand?".

His chest tightened.

More faces emerged from the haze.

Victor Costa, his father, stepped forward.

"I was killed because of you."

David's mouth opened, but no sound came.

The rope creaked above him.

Felipe, his grandfather, was there too, staring. Bleeding.

"You didn't save me," he said in a quiet voice. "You could have stopped it. You could have warned me."

David's legs went weak.

Behind them stood Molly and Rachel, dressed in white, smeared in dirt and blood from the Red Earth.

"You left us there," Molly said, eyes full of betrayal. "You just watched."

From the shadows behind them, a robed figure emerged, unfurling a scroll.

"David Costa... your sins have found you."

A bell rang, dull and final.

"Negligence. Abandonment. Cowardice."

The crowd chanted, voices rising:

"Guilty. Guilty. Guilty."

The rope dropped.

His feet lifted.

The sky turned black.

And as the noose tightened, David's last sight was Andrea, smiling, her eyes glowing red.

And next to her...

A Bald Man, whispering something only David could hear.

"You always run."

Darkness closed in around him.

And then the lights flickered.

Molly blinked.

She was in an office.

Fluorescent lights buzzed softly above her.

Phones rang. Keyboards clicked.

People bustled around her in business attire, holding coffee mugs and files, chatting like any normal day.

"Hey, Molly, can you sign off on this?" a woman asked as she passed by, smiling.

Molly frowned. "What? I—"

She didn't know these people.

She didn't even know how she got here.

She looked down.

She was wearing office clothes.

A visitor badge clipped to her shirt: Molly Costa – Consultant.

What the hell?

She walked toward a window.

The sun was bright. The sky was crystal blue.

But as she looked down...

She was high.

Way too high.

Skyscrapers below looked like toys.

The street was a blur of motion.

She backed away, her stomach twisting.

Then, a jolt.

The building shuddered, just once.

Like something massive had hit it.

The floor rattled slightly under her feet.

Coffee cups tipped. Files slid.

"What was that?" someone asked from across the room.

"Probably an earthquake," another replied, too casually.

"Felt more like an explosion," someone muttered.

Molly's blood ran cold.

She turned, walked past a nearby desk, eyes scanning the scattered papers.

A fax dated in bold at the top.

Tuesday, September 11, 2001.

Her heart stopped.

No.

She turned to a man sipping coffee near the break room.

"What floor are we on?" she asked.

He shrugged. "107th floor. Why?"

Her legs weakened.

Her breath shortened.

She looked around at all the people smiling, laughing, going about their day.

Oblivious.

"We have to go," she said. "We have to get out. Right now."

Someone laughed. "Relax, Molly. We've got meetings until noon. You'll be fine."

Another jolt.

The lights flickered.

Distant screams echoed from down the hall.

She turned and bolted for the exit.

The stairwell door. Locked.

"Why won't it open!?" she screamed, pounding on it.

"Why won't it—"

A shadow passed the window.

People began crowding at the glass.

One woman gasped, dropping her coffee.

Another clutched her face.

"There's another plane—"

Molly spun.

Inside the glass, her reflection stood frozen, wide-eyed and pale.

And just behind it, standing calmly in the room's center, was a Bald Man.

His arms were crossed. His smile was thin. Cold.

He didn't shout. He didn't move.

He just looked at her through the glass and said,

"You already know what's coming.

You're always too late, soldier.

You can't help anybody."

The lights died.

The floor dropped.
Everything went black.

Chapter 5

The Battles Seen and Unseen

Andrea and Todd sat in the car across the street from the house, engine off, windows cracked.

Andrea leaned forward, her eyes fixed on the porch light.

"I count four inside," she muttered. "Josh, David, Molly. And Leanne."

Todd gripped the steering wheel tighter. "So? They're inside. Let's just go in and handle it."

Andrea shot him a sharp look. "Don't be stupid. Josh and David could take you down if they saw you coming."

He scoffed. "Please. I'm trained."

Andrea leaned closer, her voice low. "And Leanne? Don't let the retired-lunch-lady routine fool you. She'll gut you before you blink. She's not just dangerous. She's vicious when she needs to be."

Todd blinked at her. "You're serious."

"We've got one gun, Todd. That's not enough. Not for four of them. And if they already know we're out here..."

The porch light flickered. A strange laugh echoed faintly from inside.

Todd's expression tightened. "Okay. Fine. We'll get another car, more cash, and another weapon."

Andrea nodded. "Now you're thinking clearly."

As they drove away, Shannon stood at the front window of the house she shared with Josh, just down the street from Leanne's. She had been watching them, Andrea and Todd, parked out front. Then slowly pulling away.

Josh had told her he needed to check on Leanne. But now he wasn't answering her calls or texts.

Frowning, she grabbed her phone and made her way down the block. As she reached Leanne's front yard, she spotted Molly's car parked in the driveway beside Leanne's.

The lights inside flickered. She heard strange sounds, soft laughter... and maybe even low, distant screams?

Shannon stepped up to the door and tried the knob, but it wouldn't budge.

Heart racing, unsure what to do, she called Andri.

"Did you recognize the people watching the house? Could it have been Andrea?" Andri asked.

"No. They were a young couple, maybe mid-twenties. What should I do?" Shannon's voice was tight with worry.

"Shannon, go back home. Stay inside," Andri said firmly. "If Andrea finds out where Leanne lives, she'll recognize you, and she's dangerous. Meanwhile, keep trying to reach Josh. I'll see what I can do from this end."

Drew, having overheard the conversation on speaker, spoke up. "Andri, I don't want you going there alone. I'd go myself, but I don't want to leave you here with your mom and the kids."

Andri stood up from the chair. "I'll need time alone. I'm going to the bedroom. Drew, try to keep the kids downstairs for as long as you can."

Drew looked at her, brows pinched. "Okay... but what are you going to do?"

She reached for his hand and held it. "The only thing I can do. I'll have to connect with Leanne through remote viewing."

He hesitated. "You mean, like... see her without being there?"

She nodded. "It's a way of tuning in, focusing beyond the physical. If something's happening in that house, I need to see it from the inside, even if I can't be there myself."

Andri settled into the armchair in their bedroom. It was quiet. She closed her eyes and took a few minutes to drop herself into a deeper state.

With intention, the images came, fleeting at first. But as they sharpened, she focused on Leanne's living room. Almost immediately, she could see it: the couch, the damaged wall. She felt it too: malevolent energy, thick and pressing.

She shifted her focus to the dining room. That's where she saw them, all four of them, seated at the table in some kind of trance-like state. The lights above flickered unnaturally. Andri could see the terror etched into their faces, and she felt it, a wave of raw fear pulsing from all four of them.

Something was controlling them.

Andri could sense it. Leanne was the conduit. Whatever this presence was, it was using Leanne as the anchor... feeding through her... bending the others' minds. She knew intuitively, they were trapped in hallucinations, terrifying and dangerous.

She had to connect with Leanne. And fast.

Andri focused harder, but something was pushing back. Blocking her.

She gritted her teeth and stubbornly demanded entry. She would not be denied.

Then—suddenly, there she was. Leanne.

"Andri? Is it really you?" Leanne asked, suspicious. Rightfully so. The Bald Man had deceived her before.

Andri kept her tone calm and steady. "Leanne, see me. Look at me."

She imagined reaching her hand out and continued, "Take my hand, sister. Do it now. There's not a lot of time."

Leanne looked around, confused, searching the endless gray abyss that surrounded her.

She hesitated.

Then... Leanne reached out.

But something else moved too. A dark, flowy figure, shadowed and shifting, slipping between them. Trying to break the connection.

"Leanne, ignore it," Andri urged. "Remember what Nancy Lewis told you the last time they tried to take you. You are stronger than it. Tenfold."

Nancy Lewis was a hypnotist who specialized in removing spirit attachments. She worked closely with the paranormal investigation community, where attachments were a common hazard. Leanne had once been affected by such a presence, low clinging energy that wouldn't let go. Nancy had stepped in and successfully helped her reclaim her peace.

Leanne narrowed her eyes at the shadow. With sudden authority, she commanded it to move aside. It did.

As she touched the image of Andri's hand, a surge of energy rushed through her. She knew it was real.

"Andri," she whispered.

"Leanne, demand they release you. Now. Let them know you've re-claimed your reality."

Leanne obeyed.

The moment she did, the connection snapped.

Andri's eyes flew open.

She sat in silence, heart racing, unsure if it had worked, if Leanne had broken free.

⊶◆⊷

Todd's grip on the steering wheel was tighter than necessary. They'd driven only a few blocks, but the silence between them hung heavy, like fog.

Andrea stared out the passenger window, arms crossed. Her mind still back at that house. "We shouldn't have left," she muttered.

Todd exhaled hard. "We didn't have a choice. Something was off. You saw the lights. Heard that laughter. That wasn't just people inside having a chat. That was... wrong."

"Todd, let's go back," Andrea said. "The longer we wait, the greater the chance we'll run into problems."

Todd slowed the car and pulled over. "I thought you said we needed more weapons. Now you want to charge in?"

Andrea glanced back at the zip ties in the rear seat. "Yeah, but you've got police experience. I can hold all four of them with one gun. We've got zip ties. You tie Josh, Molly, and Leanne. Leave David to me. I want to zip-tie his ass... like he did to me."

Todd looked at her. "Fine, do whatever you want with David. Hell. I was planning to disappear him myself. But Josh? He's mine. I want to return him to custody. I want it on record that before I retired, Chief Edmonds caught Josh Coleman."

Andrea smirked. "Let's go back."

Todd made a U-turn and drove back toward Leanne's house. They parked across the street. The lights inside still flickered, though not as wildly as before. But they spotted Leanne, David, and Josh standing on the lawn. They glanced at each other, suspicious.

Without a word, they watched from the shadows, waiting for the right moment.

Minutes earlier, inside the house, all four of them had opened their eyes at once. The dark laughter was gone. No more doll costumes, no tea sets. No twisted visions from other places and times. Just the four of them, sitting at the kitchen table, shaken but awake.

Leanne looked around. "Is everyone alright?"

Josh jumped up. "Mom, are you?" He stepped over to her and hugged her tightly. Tears ran freely down both their faces.

David turned to Molly, who was holding her injured leg. "Come on, let's get out of this house." He scooped her up and headed for the door.

Josh did the same with Leanne.

"Josh, I can walk," Leanne said with a weak smile.

Josh didn't smile. He just wanted to get them the hell out of there.

Outside, David grabbed a porch chair and set it on the lawn, gently placing Molly into it. The others stood around, staring at the house, trying to make sense of what had just happened.

Leanne and Josh both knew. It was another attack. The Bald Man again. It had been years since the last time. And this time, it was worse.

Leanne could still feel his energy. It clung to the house like humidity. The lights still flickered.

The presence hadn't left.

She wondered how she'd ever be able to rid the house of him. But for now, they were safe.

"Aunt Leanne," David asked, "what the hell just happened to us in there?"

"Yeah," Molly murmured. "That was way worse than the Red Earth."

Leanne choked up. "I'm sorry you had to go through that. I feel so bad—"

Josh cut her off. "No, Mom. Don't. It's not your fault."

Then he turned to David and Molly. "We'll explain everything, I promise. *Just*... not right now. Mom needs time. We all do."

David nodded.

Leanne pulled out her phone. "I need to call Andri." As she dialed, she walked toward the garage, away from the others.

Molly turned to David. "You ready to leave?"

"Yeah. Wait in the car. I just need to talk to Josh for a minute."

Molly nodded and limped to the car, easing herself into the driver's seat.

David walked over to Josh. As the two of them talked, Leanne returned, walking briskly toward them.

"Andri says we should leave the area now. Whatever was here. It's still lingering. Josh, I'll stay at your place until we figure out how to clear it."

Josh nodded silently.

Then, from behind them:

"Hands up. And keep them up."

They froze. Unsure if it was real, but unwilling to take a chance, they obeyed.

"Now walk toward the house. Slowly. And keep those hands up."

They hesitated.

Josh's gut twisted. Andrea and Chief Edmonds were after them... but the voice sounded too young. Still, he recognized that accent, Texan, unmistakably.

Then David called out, "Andrea? Is that you?"

A sharp laugh followed. "My son, always so clever. You take after me in that respect."

David frowned. She sounded different.

Josh narrowed his eyes. "Show me the gun."

Andrea replied smugly, "Turn around. Look for yourself."

They all turned slowly.

Josh and David's eyes widened.

Leanne gasped.

The dark energy of the Bald Man seeped from the house like smoke. He was furious, seething. Leanne could feel it. The closer they got to the front door, the stronger it became.

His full face, deep-set eyes, a sharp hook nose, dark circles etched beneath, only made him more grotesque. He wore nothing but a long black cloak. His focus was fixed on Leanne. The hatred he felt for her was personal, ancient. He had tried to take her before, twice, and both times she'd escaped.

Something always protected her. Helped her. But one day, one opening, one misstep. That's all he needed. When she was vulnerable again, he'd dive in without hesitation.

But this time, he hadn't gone for her directly. This time, he targeted the ones she loved. It had made her weaker. More exposed. He had been close. But someone had helped her again. The connection had been blocked. Closed. Just like the others. And now they were leaving the house.

He watched them gather on the lawn.

He also watched two strangers approach, demanding they return inside.

Then Leanne spoke. "Whatever you're looking for, you can find it right here. It's too dangerous to go back into that house."

Andrea smirked. "And why is that?"

Before Leanne could respond, David stepped forward. "Because, Andrea, there's a Bald Man. A very evil spirit inside that house. He just tormented us. That's why we had to get out. So if you're here for me, take me right here. But I'm not stepping foot back in that house. And while you're far from being my favorite person, I'd suggest you stay out of it too."

Josh looked directly at them. "What the hell did you both do... to look young?" he asked.

Andrea and Todd ignored him.

Andrea scoffed at David's warning. "A Bald Man? Really? Can't you guys come up with something better than that?"

Todd glanced at her warily. "Andrea, let's just take them now."

Without waiting for her reply, he stepped forward. "On your knees," he ordered, pointing at Leanne and Josh.

He reached into the bag and pulled out zip-ties.

David's eyes locked with Josh's. Something had to be done. Now.

As Todd reached to bind Josh's wrists, Josh suddenly lunged, grabbing Andrea's legs and knocking her flat. The gun flew from her hand.

Todd dove toward it. David kicked him square in the face, sending him sprawling. Andrea scrambled for the weapon, but Josh got to it first.

Andrea squirmed, kicking wildly. Josh pinned her down with a laugh.

"Mom, hand me the zip-ties," Josh said.

Leanne tossed them over and helped hold Andrea still as Josh worked to bind her wrists.

Meanwhile, David finished zip-tying Todd's wrists and ankles with the remaining ties. He grinned.

"I've outsmarted you once before, when you were supposed to be smarter and wiser. And now, as a young man, when you're supposed to be faster and stronger. I've kicked your ass, or... well, your face. Same thing."

Todd lay there, silent and defeated.

From the shadows, the Bald Man watched. His eyes glowed red.

He focused his energy, his rage, on the zip-tie in Josh's hand.

He wanted Andrea to lead them back into the house. So he decided to help Andrea.

Just as Josh began to secure Andrea's wrist, the plastic snapped into pieces.

"Dammit," Josh muttered.

David turned just in time as the gun slid across the ground, straight toward Andrea.

He dove for it.

Too late.

Andrea grabbed it, flipped onto her side, and aimed it straight at Josh.

"Step back," she snapped, motioning for David to follow. "And Leanne, you're coming inside with us."

"No, Andrea. You don't want to go in there," David said, alarmed.

Andrea turned the gun toward him. "What? Are you afraid of some stupid Bald Man spirit?"

David stared at her. "Yes."

Andrea scoffed. "You're a grown man afraid of some dumbass ghost with mommy issues? He probably couldn't get laid when he was alive, and now he floats around, terrorizing people for attention. What a *loser.*"

Leanne didn't know if the Bald Man had heard her.

But something told her he had.
From the shadows, he waited, hungry.
And hoped Andrea would step into the house.
Because he had heard every word.

Chapter 6

The Box and Red Rocks

Andrea kept the gun aimed at them as she led them inside.

Leanne and David moved slowly, hands raised, stopping just past the doorway.

"Keep going," Andrea ordered, stepping further into the hallway.

Leanne's stomach tightened. The house felt different, heavier. The air throbbed with something dark and alive.

Andrea only laughed.

"See? Nothing," she said, walking backward. "No ghost. No Bald Man. Just your creepy little house. You people are—"

She stumbled.

Her heel hit something solid. She spun around.

A large wooden box had appeared behind her. Quiet. Waiting.

Andrea turned, eyes narrowing. "What the hell is—"

Before she could finish, she was yanked backward into it.

The box looked open. It looked like she could walk out at any time.

But she couldn't.

She was trapped, body flush against invisible walls. She pounded her fists. Screamed.

And then she fired.

The bullet ricocheted inside the unseen walls and struck her in the leg. She howled in pain.

Leanne lunged forward, but couldn't move. Neither could David.

The house held them there. Frozen.

From outside, Josh, having heard the first scream, ran to the door. He stopped cold in the entryway, paralyzed.

Behind him, Shannon and Molly appeared.

"What's happening?" Molly whispered, but her voice caught as her legs gave out beneath her. She fell to her knees, unable to crawl away.

Shannon gasped. "I can't... move..."

They could all see.

But none of them could act.

Andrea continued to thrash inside the box, now howling in disbelief.

"You think this scares me?!" Andrea screamed. "I'm not afraid!"

And then, with a sickening final groan—the box crushed inward.

The creak of wood. The metallic groan of unseen hinges. The steady collapse.

Andrea's body bent forward involuntarily as the invisible walls closed in.

Leanne begged, "Stop! Please stop!"

David clenched his jaw. "Don't look," he said, though no one could look away.

The box crushed inward.

Andrea screamed once more, high, animalistic, then fell silent.

Bones cracked.

Blood oozed.

And then... silence.

The box compressed until it was no larger than a shoebox, then crumpled in on itself and vanished.

All that remained was the blood, dripping, slow and deliberate, onto the hardwood floor.

Todd lay on the porch where Josh had dragged him, just moments before running inside at the sound of the first scream.

Now he stared at the open door, heart pounding.

He could hear it: Andrea's screams, wild with terror.

There were crashes, strange shifting sounds, and the sharp ring of a gunshot.

Then another scream, shrill and broken.

It was Andrea.

What the hell is happening in there?

Are they killing her?

Am I next?

But as he strained to lift his head, he caught sight of the others: Leanne, David, Josh, Shannon, even Molly. Frozen, motionless, their eyes locked on something inside the hallway.

They weren't moving, weren't attacking, weren't doing anything.

They were just... watching.

And from the looks on their faces. Whatever they were seeing wasn't just horrifying.

It was unnatural.

A chill ran down Todd's spine.

This isn't them, he thought. This is something else.

Just then, he looked up and saw a black cat. It walked slowly, steps measured, toward the fence and leapt onto the ledge.

Before it jumped onto the roof, the cat paused, turned, and stared directly at him.

Pale blue eyes locked with his, freezing him in place.

He found himself unable to look away until the cat finally turned, breaking the trance.

It leapt onto the roof, and the moment it did, everyone burst out of the house.

The paralysis that had held them inside shattered.

Inside, the Bald Man peered through the window, seething.

Again, something had intervened. Something had helped them.

He didn't know how, but he would fix it.

He would make another box.

For Leanne.

Outside on the lawn, David dragged Todd away from the porch.

Josh approached. "What are we going to do with him?"

David shook his head. "We have to send him back."

Josh glanced down at Todd, who lay sprawled on the grass.

Todd nodded quickly. "Yes. Please. Send me back."

Josh chuckled mockingly. "Looking like that? You think you're going to just slip back into your life as Chief Edmonds?"

Todd's face drained of color.

The realization hit hard. He couldn't.

Not like this.

Not as a man in his twenties.

"The mirror," Todd said suddenly. "Andrea had a mirror that changed us, and…" he stopped.

His voice caught.

"She had it on her, didn't she?" David asked.

Todd looked at the house. "Yeah… is she still in there?"

Josh opened his mouth, then closed it.

Still shaken by what they'd witnessed, he just looked away.

David, picking up on Josh's silence, answered instead. "No. She's not there anymore. If she had the mirror, then it's gone."

Todd stared, confused. "Look, I know something bad happened. I heard…"

Then he noticed David turning away.

Josh walked off.

David exhaled. "Yes. She's dead. But she's not there."

"Her body's got to be in there. The mirror was in her pocket," Todd insisted.

David didn't argue, just stared. "I told you. She's dead. And there's nothing left of her."

Andri and Drew arrived, joining Leanne, Molly, and Josh on the lawn. One by one, they began sharing what had happened.

"Andri," Leanne said, "I thought it was an illusion. Like before."

She shook her head. "It wasn't."

"It's still in the house?" Andri asked.

Leanne nodded. "It took hold again, stronger this time. I'm not sure what to do."

"It's getting stronger, feeding off fear," Andri said. "What happened to Andrea supercharged it."

We have to find a way to get it out of the house. But for now, we need to leave. It's far too dangerous to stay here."

Molly sobbed against Josh's shoulder. "I know I'm not acting brave. I'm just crying like some scared girl. But after what we saw in that house... that box thing...I just—"

Josh turned to her gently. "Hey. You have every right to cry right now. You were brave when it counted, like a soldier standing tall through all of it. What we *saw*... what we lived through, that takes a toll. Now that we're out of it, we're all trying to let go in our own way. So yeah, cry. Break down. You're still our brave soldier girl."

As the women headed toward Josh and Shannon's house, David and Drew caught up with Andri.

"We're taking Todd to Mystic Crossroads," David said. "Josh and I are going to ask Tanya if she can help send him back."

"Please be careful," Andri said, her expression filled with concern.

Drew placed an arm around her shoulder, leaned in, and kissed her cheek. "We'll be fine."

David glanced around. "Where are the kids?" he asked, looking from Andri to Drew and back again.

"Don't worry," Drew replied. "Bobby Wren and his wife, Flora, are at the house with them."

David nodded, relieved. "Ah, your work partner?"

"Yeah," Drew said with a nod.

— ◦ —

Todd, now sitting up on the front lawn, glanced toward the porch and froze.

The black cat was back.

This time, it was walking slowly along the porch rail. With a closer view, Todd noticed its sleek, shiny coat rippling gently in the breeze. The cat moved toward the front door, then paused again, locking eyes with him.

He held the gaze for only a moment before quickly looking away. He refused to be caught in another trance.

He looked around. Josh was standing on the sidewalk, absorbed in his phone, but the others weren't in sight.

Todd turned back just in time to see the cat approach the front door. It paused, hesitating.

Then, the door slowly creaked open.

Todd blinked. *What the hell?*

Don't go in there, cat, he thought.

The cat stepped inside.

The door slammed shut behind it.

Josh, startled by the slam, ran to Todd. Without hesitation, he grabbed him by the arm and pulled him farther away from the house, onto the driveway.

Drew and David rushed over, alarmed.

"What the hell happened?" Drew asked.

Todd, still wide-eyed, said, "A cat. There was a cat on the porch. The door opened on its own... it walked in... and then it slammed shut."

"A cat?" David repeated. "A fuckin' cat? Are you serious?"

The three men looked at each other, brows furrowed, expressions darkening.

Suddenly, a deep rumbling sound rolled through the ground beneath their feet.

They all froze.

It came from the house.

The walls seemed to vibrate, the porch boards groaning under unseen pressure.

The very air around them thickened, like the storm before a strike.

Then—BOOM.

The front windows shattered outward, glass exploding into the yard like sharp rain.

The door blew open, not in a swing, but with a forceful swoosh, like a vacuum releasing pressure.

A gust of wind rushed out, powerful enough to whip their clothes and steal the breath from their lungs.

Then... silence.

The house stood still.

No humming. No flickering lights. No weight in the air.

Just... stillness.

Josh stared at the doorway—his body rigid, breath caught in his throat.

Then, slowly, he exhaled.

"He's gone," he said, barely above a whisper. "He's really gone."

David looked at the shattered windows, the open doorway, and then toward the empty porch.

"Whatever that cat did…" he murmured, shaking his head. "God, I don't even want to know. But it worked."

Josh pulled out his phone and called Leanne.

"Mom," he said, his voice low but certain. "He's left the house. The Bald Man is gone."

He explained what had happened, and within minutes, the women made their way back.

Andri, Leanne, Drew, and Josh approached the house together.

Carefully, they stepped over the shattered glass, then over the front door, now lying flat and splintered on the porch.

They crossed the threshold slowly, eyes scanning every corner as they entered the house.

From the driveway, David, Molly, Shannon, and Todd watched, silent, tense, waiting.

A few minutes later, they stepped back outside.

Smiles had returned to their faces, relieved, cautious… but real.

David spoke first. "Everything okay?"

Leanne nodded. "It's clean. There's nothing here. You can feel it: the shift in energy. They're gone."

Andri added, "Completely gone. It's like the air can breathe again."

"And Andrea's… the blood?" David asked hesitantly.

"Also gone," Andri answered.

Everyone exhaled a little easier.

But then Drew looked back at the wrecked porch, the broken windows, and the front door still lying on its side.

"Well," he said with a half-smile, "they didn't exactly leave things tidy."

Josh laughed under his breath.

Drew continued, "Don't worry. I'll have Bobby come board up the windows and door, take some measurements. Once we get back from Lincoln, I'll fix everything."

Leanne looked at him gratefully. "Thank you."

He gave a quick nod. "We'll take care of it. You're not alone in this."

Josh glanced back at Todd.

"You parked across the street, right?" he asked. "That black sedan, yours?"

Todd hesitated. "Yeah, well... technically. I borrowed it. From a parking lot. Without asking."

Josh froze. "Hell no. You're not leaving a stolen car in front of my mom's house.

That thing needs to be gone. Now."

Drew raised a brow. "Okay, well... who's driving it out of here? He sure as hell can't."

"I'm not driving it," David said flatly. "I'm not touching that mess."

"Nobody wants to drive a stolen car," Drew muttered, "especially not from a scene like this."

Josh turned back to Todd. "Then he's gonna have to."

He crouched down and pulled the last of the plastic ties from Todd's wrists, letting them fall to the ground.

Josh leaned in, voice low and firm. "You try anything stupid... you'll wish the cops caught you first." He paused. "Besides, where the hell are you gonna go?"

Todd looked up at him, exhausted, broken, and very aware of his options.

He sat up, rubbing his wrist.

"I'm not going anywhere," he muttered. "You don't have to worry about me. I'm not trying to run. I just want to get my ass back to where I belong. This place? It's been way too crazy for me. I'm done. Seriously."

David looked at the car across the street, then back at Todd. "Well, he's driving. But who the hell's riding with him?"

Josh frowned. "You riding with him?"

Drew shook his head. "Nope."

Josh threw up his hands. "Yeah, I'm not climbing into a stolen car with this guy."

David sighed, glanced at the sky like he was praying for patience. "Fine. I'll ride with him."

He looked at Todd with a flat stare. "But if he gets pulled over, I didn't know a damn thing about the car, got it?"

Todd raised his hands in mock surrender. "Understood."

They were thirty minutes outside of Lincoln when Todd and David ditched the car on a remote country road, driving it a few yards down a dirt path and hiding it behind the trees.

Drew had insisted they walk nearly a mile to meet him at his truck, just in case they were being followed.

In the truck, David and Todd sat in the back seat. David still didn't trust him, so he kept a watchful eye.

"What good is it now for me to go back if I can't even be myself?" Todd said anxiously. "I won't be able to collect my retirement. I won't have any provable skills, and nowhere to live."

Josh, annoyed, turned back from the front passenger seat. "Do what I had to do when I was stuck in your shithole of a world. Live with the homeless. Steal clothes. Let the charity workers feed you."

Todd narrowed his eyes. "The only thing better about this world is the sky and the air. But I've never seen or experienced so much strange shit. Fucked up shit."

Josh snapped, "Well, that's what happens when you get yourself tangled up with someone like Andrea."

Drew chimed in sarcastically, "Hey, at least you've got your youth back. You can start all over."

Before Todd could respond, Josh's phone buzzed. It was Shannon. "Babe, where are you?"

"We're just getting into Lincoln now. Have you been able to get a hold of Tanya yet?" Josh asked.

"No. She's not answering her phone or her texts. I'm getting worried. But I didn't just call for that."

As they neared Mystic Crossroads, the truck grew quiet.

Josh realized everyone could hear Shannon's voice through the phone, so he switched it to speaker.

"Why else?" he asked, now concerned.

"The weather. There've been reports of bad weather in that area, Josh. They're saying possible tornadoes," Shannon said.

Just then, David and Drew's phones buzzed.

It was Andri and Leanne.

They didn't need to answer. They already knew why Andri and Leanne were calling.

No one had noticed the dark, gray sky creeping in. But now they all looked out the windows.

Silence.

"Shit," David and Drew said in unison.

Sedona, Arizona

Tanya was transported to a spot in Sedona, but she wasn't sure exactly. It looked like a construction site, equipment scattered around, a barbed-wire fence enclosing the area with a sign that read: DO NOT ENTER BEYOND THIS POINT.

To the left of it, another sign: NO TRESPASSING.

She looked around, trying to understand why Anio had sent her here. In the distance, red rock mountains stood tall, silent sentinels watching over the land.

She spotted a large, flat rock and lowered herself onto it slowly, still glancing around. Reaching into her bag, she pulled out Anio's map and spread it across her lap.

Tanya studied the map, then looked up, scanning the terrain. The mountains, the ridges... everything matched. Just as Anio had drawn it.

This is it. This was where she was supposed to be.

She took a deep breath, closed her eyes, and let the energy settle into her.

Peaceful. Serene.

Joe had been looking forward to this tee time all week. Contra Costa Country Club was exclusive, pristine, the kind of course he'd always dreamed of playing. The sky was clear, the greens flawless, and for once, his swing was actually decent.

They had just pulled up to the next hole when his phone buzzed.

His screen flashed: Tanya.

He frowned. *Tanya?* How did she even get his number?

"Hang on," he said to the guys, climbing out of the golf cart. He circled around to the far side, away from the group, and answered the call.

Her voice came through, calm but urgent. "Joe, I need you to meet me in Sedona. Anio's going to handle the transport."

He blinked, glancing back toward the cart. His buddies were still laughing, completely unaware.

"You're serious?" he asked, lowering his voice. "And how do you even have my—"

But the air had already begun to change, lighter, charged. He exhaled and gripped his golf club as the world around him shimmered.

Moments later, he was gone.

Tanya sat quietly on the rock, the crumpled map still in her lap. The air was peaceful, untouched, until something shifted and caught her attention.

She looked up.

About ten feet in front of her, the air had begun to bend. It shimmered like heat rising off desert pavement, only denser, alive, as if the air itself were breathing. It pulsed outward in slow, mesmerizing ripples, warping the red rocks behind it.

She knew what it was. A portal.

A moment later, Joe stepped through it, one foot hesitating mid-air like he wasn't quite sure what surface he'd land on. He was still holding a golf club, wearing cleats and a collared shirt. Completely out of place against the raw, earthy terrain of Sedona.

He blinked, turning in a slow circle as if he half-expected a crowd of golfers to be waiting behind him.

Then he spotted her.

Relief washed across his face. "Oh, thank God, I thought I was about to tee off in the Twilight Zone."

Tanya smiled, rising to her feet. "Nice outfit."

Joe looked down at his khakis and visor, then back at her. "Yeah, well, I wasn't exactly briefed on the dress code for interdimensional travel."

Joe looked around, the golf club still in his hand, like some kind of cosmic joke. "Okay. I'm here. Sedona. So... what's going on?"

Tanya stood near the edge of the construction site, wind brushing strands of hair across her face. She didn't answer right away.

Instead, she turned and looked out over the partially built structures.

"You see that building in the center?" she asked.

He nodded. "Yeah."

"That's going to be the new Mystic Crossroads."

Joe's brows lifted. "Wait, the Mystic Crossroads?"

Tanya nodded. "The one in Nebraska will be no more. Don't ask. I don't have the answer." She gestured to the surrounding construction. "Those houses are being built for the Perez family. Nora's children. The Perez family are marked as guardians."

Joe froze. "For... us?"

"Yes," she said, watching his reaction. "It's yours now. All of you. This land, the shop, the portals. You'll run it. Guard it."

Joe turned slowly, taking it all in, the red rock horizon wrapped around them like a painted dome. "This is big, Tanya. Like... huge."

"It is," she said quietly. "Anio's crew will arrive soon to finish the work. A representative will take my scrolls and maps, get everything filed: the deeds, the transfers. It's already in motion."

Joe looked back at her, suspicion flickering behind his eyes. "And what about you? Where do you fit into all of this?"

Tanya gave a soft smile and looked away. "For now... I'm just here to help start things off."

Joe looked at her, clearly confused. "So... my family is going to be guarding portals? Do they even know?"

Tanya smiled faintly. "I haven't told anyone. Except you."

His eyes drifted toward the unfinished homes, then back to the red rock horizon.

The weight of it hit slowly, like thunder rumbling from far away.

"That means..." he said softly, more to himself than to her, "we're all moving to Sedona?"

He looked out into the distance.

A few miles away, the city of Sedona nestled against the red rock horizon.

The sun cast long amber shadows across the cliffs, bathing the land in gold.

He turned to her slowly, his expression uncertain. "Tanya," he said, his voice low, "can I ask you something?"

She glanced over, a little surprised by his hesitation. "Of course."

He scratched the back of his neck. "I've heard this place... it's known for a lot of UFO sightings?"

Her eyes lit up. "Oh, absolutely," she said with a soft chuckle. "Sedona's kind of a hotspot for that."

People come from all over hoping to see something in the skies."

Joe nodded slowly, his gaze drifting back to the horizon. "Yeah," he murmured, mostly to himself. "That's what I was afraid of."

Just then, they watched as dust rose into the air. Vehicles kicking up dirt as they approached the site.

Tanya smiled. "They're here."

Chapter 7

When the Wind Came

Engines hummed in the distance, growing louder with each passing second. Dust rolled in long arcs across the dry earth as a caravan of dark trucks and utility vans crested the ridge. They moved with purpose, like they knew exactly where to go. Because they did.

Joe stepped forward instinctively, shielding his eyes with his hand. The first vehicle came to a halt at the edge of the development. Doors opened. Men and women in matching dark gray uniforms began to step out; silent, efficient, and somehow... not entirely ordinary.

They didn't speak. Not yet. They moved in sync, like gears in a well-oiled machine. Within minutes, crates were being unloaded, scaffolding assembled, blueprints unrolled directly onto the hoods of trucks.

Tanya stood still, watching. "They'll finish quickly," she murmured. "They always do."

Joe turned to her, his voice lower now. "Who are these people, really?"

"They're builders," she said finally. "Of places and... of possibilities."

Joe shielded his eyes from the sunlight, watching as the first vehicle, a sleek black SUV, came to a slow stop in front of the unfinished structure.

Tanya stood beside him, her posture calm, almost reverent.

From the SUV, a sharply dressed woman stepped out, her movements precise and efficient. Her dark sunglasses reflected the red rocks behind them, and a sleek binder was tucked beneath her arm.

"Ms. Varela?" Tanya called out, her voice clipped but polite.

She stepped forward with a slight nod. "We've been expecting you."

The woman offered a brief smile before turning to Joe. "Mr. Perez, I'm here on behalf of Anio. We're finalizing the transfers. Your family will receive the keys at the beginning of next month."

Joe blinked, caught off guard by the formality of it all.

The woman continued, flipping open her binder. "There will be eight residential units built behind the main structure. Enough for your immediate family: Nora's children, and the grandchildren. Your names are on the deeds."

The woman handed Tanya a manila envelope. Without a word, she handed it to Tanya, who then passed it to Joe.

Joe looked back at Tanya, searching her face for answers.

"This is for your family," Tanya said. "Keep it sealed. Don't open it until everyone's moved in and you've had your first family meeting. They're building a private chamber behind the store just for that. It's soundproof, protected. That's where you'll open it."

Joe looked down at the envelope. It was heavier than he expected. "What's in it?"

Tanya's expression softened. "Maps, details... information about the four portals. Their locations, their purposes. Things the family will need to understand when the time comes."

His brow furrowed. "There's four?"

"Yes," she said.

Joe glanced up sharply, but Tanya was already looking back at the red rocks. Her posture had changed, calmer now, like something in her had already let go.

"I need to go back to the ranch in Superior," she said suddenly.

She nodded. "It's where my family lived. There's space there. A barn house I used to rent out. It's empty now. I want to spend time there."

"I want the whole family to come there," she continued. "Once they're settled in Sedona. After the move, after the dust settles, gather them. Invite everyone to the ranch. I want to see them all there."

Joe gave a slow, heavy nod. "Okay. I'll make sure they come."

He smiled faintly and stepped back, as if releasing him. "Now it's time for you to go back to where you were."

Joe blinked. "The golf course? I'm not even sure if they're still there."

"Oh, they will be," she said with a knowing look. "For you, it'll be like you never left. Time has a way of holding its breath when the right people are watching."

—◦—

Meanwhile, back in Lincoln, Nebraska, just outside the weathered walls of Mystic Crossroads. The wind was picking up fast.

Debris skipped across the road like forgotten leaves, and the sky churned with a shade of gray none of them had ever seen before. Drew tightened his grip on the steering wheel, eyes flicking between the road and the darkening horizon.

He couldn't check his phone, but he didn't need to. Everyone else in the truck already had the same uneasy look etched across their faces.

Drew gripped the wheel tighter. "We're almost there. Should we pull over?"

"No," David said sharply. "Keep going. We need to get to the store before it hits."

Josh checked his phone. "It's coming in from the northwest. Fast-moving. No time to outrun it."

That's when they saw it.

Mystic Crossroads. Still standing.

"Tanya... if she's in there, we need to find her," Josh said, his voice tight with concern.

Drew veered off the road and into the parking lot, tires skidding across the gravel.

"Let's move!" David shouted as they came to a stop. "Everyone out!"

They leapt from the truck, jackets whipping in the wind, their voices swallowed by the roar of thunder.

Drew ran to the back cellar door and grabbed the heavy latch. It was locked.

Then—click!

The latch gave way. The door creaked open.

They all froze.

The front windows had been blown inward. Glass littered the floor in jagged puddles. Shelves had toppled. Broken merchandise covered the tile. Wind screamed through the open doorway, slamming what remained of the front door against the wall.

The entire building moaned as if it, too, knew the end was near.

They ran inside, splitting up, shouting Tanya's name.

"She's not answering," Josh yelled over the storm. "No calls, no texts. We were hoping she'd be here."

"We can't use the portal without her," David said, scanning the destroyed interior. "She guards the portal. She knows how to guide it."

"She's gotta be here somewhere!" Drew called out, disappearing down the back hallway.

Outside, structures nearby were crumbling. The wind had gone from angry to feral.

"GO!" Drew shouted from the hall. "Get out! This place isn't going to hold!"

Josh nodded, yanked the front door open wider, and stepped into the gale, then turned back.

"David! Drew! Come on!"

David darted through the shadows, eyes wild. "One more pass. I have to find her!"

"Drew, move!" Josh yelled, motioning to the door. But Drew didn't move.

A loud crack split the air.

Ceiling beams groaned and collapsed.

A section of the wall gave out. Debris rained down.

Josh turned just in time to see Drew pinned beneath a heavy beam, his legs trapped under the weight.

"DREW!"

Drew gritted his teeth, trying to move. "I'm stuck," he gasped. "You need to go."

Josh dropped to his knees, gripping Drew's arms. He pulled hard, but Drew barely budged.

"I'm not leaving you here!" Josh barked.

Drew shoved him back. "If you don't go now, you won't leave at all!"

The ceiling trembled above.

"Where's David?" Josh cried out.

Drew's voice was hoarse. "Still inside... looking."

Josh staggered to his feet and turned toward the hallway.

Then he stopped.

Todd was still inside, too.

But Josh didn't care. He didn't care if Todd made it out or not.

He cared about David.

And David was still in that collapsing building.

Josh cupped his hands and screamed into the wind,

"DAVID! TANYA!"

No reply.

Only the roar of the wind... and the sound of time running out.

The store groaned above them, beams cracking, glass fracturing in its final warning.

Josh made a move toward the doorway again, but Drew threw out an arm.

"Don't," he barked. "It's coming down."

"I can't just leave him!"

"You have to!" Drew shouted. But then, a sudden crash.

Josh scrambled over, shielding Drew with his own body as more debris rained down. Drew yelled through gritted teeth, "Josh! Get out of here!" He tried to push him away. "Go!"

"There's nowhere to go," Josh said, glancing back at the truck, overturned, windows shattered.

The road was littered with twisted metal and branches. "It's all the same out there. We're in it!"

The roar of the tornado began to shift. The ground still trembled, but the sound was changing, moving, lifting.

They both looked up.

Wind still whipped around them, but the center of chaos was drifting off.

The pressure slowly released, like the breath of something monstrous being drawn away.

Silence, thick and eerie, settled in.

They froze when they heard something shuffling.

Through the haze of dust and rubble, a figure emerged. Todd.

He was limping, face streaked with blood and dirt, and in his arms...

"David!" Josh ran toward them.

Todd collapsed to his knees and carefully laid David down on the ground.

Josh's heart sank.

Blood soaked David's shirt, spreading fast from where a long shard of debris had pierced his torso.

David's eyes fluttered open.

"Hey..." he whispered.

"Stay with me, David," Josh said, kneeling beside him. "Just hang on. We've got you."

David's lips moved, but no words came.

Josh leaned closer.

Finally, David whispered, "Make sure my mom... takes care of the girls."

"You're gonna be there to take care of them yourself," Josh said, blinking fast. "Don't talk like that."

David coughed, a wet sound. "Promise me, Josh..."

His voice was breaking. "Promise me you'll take care of them. Just in case..."

Josh's jaw tightened. "We're family, David. Of course we will. But nothing's going to happen to you."

"Goddammit, Josh," David muttered, his eyes now glassy, "just say it."

Josh reached for his hand. "Okay. I promise. You hear me? I promise."

Tears welled up in his eyes. "But don't you dare leave me. Don't do it."

Behind them, Drew groaned. "Uh, guys? Still pinned here..."

Todd wiped the sweat from his brow. "On it."

He moved fast, helping Josh lift the beam and roll it off Drew's legs.

Drew winced but managed to sit up. Nothing broken, just bruises.

Josh stood, fumbling for his phone with trembling hands.

He dialed Leanne. No signal.

Tried Andri. Nothing.

Then, his phone buzzed.

A call.

Tanya.

He stared at the screen. Answered.

"Tanya?" he said, barely believing it.

Her voice was calm. "Yes, Josh. I'm here."

Of course it was her.

How had he even doubted?

Of course it was Tanya.

"Tanya?" Josh's voice cracked with disbelief. "How the hell did you get through?"

"I always get through," she said calmly. "I heard about the tornado. I called Andri, she's frantic. She said the four of you were heading toward Mystic Crossroads, and then everything went silent. No calls. No texts. Nothing."

Josh looked around at the wreckage, at David lying pale and bleeding next to him. "Yeah," he said hoarsely. "It hit us hard. We tried to find you. We thought you'd be here."

"I wasn't," Tanya replied. "And I'm glad now that I wasn't. But Josh... is everyone alright?"

Josh swallowed. "It's David. It doesn't look good. He's losing blood. We can't get him help. There's no way out. Roads are blocked. Towers are down. I don't know what to do."

There was a pause. Then Tanya's voice softened. "I'll talk to Leanne."

Josh blinked. "What? Tanya, my mom's not here. She's—"

"She'll come," Tanya said simply. "She'll know what to do."

"But how?" Josh asked, almost to himself. "How the hell is that even possible?"

Tanya didn't answer that.

Instead, she said, "Stay with him. Keep him warm. Help is coming. Trust me."

After the call ended, Josh returned to the others, his legs unsteady beneath him. Drew was kneeling beside David, holding his hand tightly, murmuring steady words meant to anchor him. Todd stood nearby, arms crossed, face tight with concern, doing what little he could to shield David from the wind and falling debris.

"Hang on, man," Drew whispered. "We've got you. Just stay with us. You're not leaving, you hear me?"

They were doing everything they could, covering him with jackets, keeping pressure on the wound, trying to keep him warm. But David's skin was pale, and the blood loss was taking its toll fast.

Then, without warning, there they were.

Leanne and Andri. Stood just a few feet away.

It was as if the storm had paused around them. No one had seen them arrive, and yet they were there, rooted to the ground in disbelief.

Andri's mouth parted in a silent gasp, the color draining from her face as she took in the sight of her son on the ground.

Leanne stood beside her, stunned, holding something tight against her chest.

The mirror.

The same mirror Anio had given her. The same mirror she'd nearly forgotten until now.

Josh rose slowly to his feet, his breath catching in his throat.

"Tanya," he muttered under his breath. "You really did get through..."

Leanne took a deep breath and exhaled slowly. Her eyes never left David as she stepped forward, lowering herself to her knees beside him. The mirror was clutched tightly to her chest, an object she had once accepted with hesitation, now seeming to pulse with purpose in her hands.

She shifted it carefully into her palm and steadied her breath.

Then, with quiet resolve, she placed her fingers on the surface. Her focus sharpened. She held David in her heart, her mind locking onto one thought: *The wound is gone. The bleeding never happened. He is whole.*

She tapped the mirror once, then slowly dragged her finger downward.

For a moment, nothing happened. Just the wind, the dust, the weight of everyone's held breath.

David stirred.

His skin, moments before drained of life, began to regain color. The deep gash in his side shimmered, and the jagged shard that had pierced him... vanished.

Gone. As if it had never been there.

The wound sealed itself completely: no blood, no scarring, not even a trace.

David's chest rose and fell rapidly. His eyes fluttered open. He was breathing hard, too weak to speak, but alive.

He looked down at himself in disbelief, then at Leanne, then back again.

Leanne kept her hand over the mirror a moment longer, grounding the last threads of energy, then gently pulled it back to her chest.

It had worked.

David was healed.

Leanne stood, still clutching the mirror to her chest.

Her voice was calm but firm. "Come on. Let's gather around. We need to get the hell out of here."

Josh blinked, overwhelmed. "Mom... how?"

She looked at him with that quiet, knowing look. "The mirror."

Without another word, everyone stepped closer. Josh helped steady David, while Drew leaned heavily on Todd for support. Andri stood just behind Leanne, her face pale but resolute.

Leanne held the mirror out before her, her fingers steady. She closed her eyes for just a moment, centered herself, then tapped her finger down the glass.

The air shimmered around them, light bending, sound distorting. The wreckage, the wind, the torn earth... all of it slipped away.

And then they were gone.

Vanished from the chaos, as if they'd never been there.

Chapter 8

The Protector Awakens

The morning sun filtered through the bedroom window, casting a soft glow across the room. A light tapping at the door pulled Andri from sleep. She opened her eyes slowly, blinking against the brightness, and turned her head to the side. Drew lay beside her, still fast asleep, his breathing steady with a faint snore. He was completely spent, just like the rest of them.

The day before had felt like a lifetime: from the madness at Leanne's house to the tornado tearing through Lincoln... It had been one of the most surreal and exhausting days any of them could remember, except maybe for the time they crossed into the red world.

Another knock.

"Yeah?" Andri called, her voice groggy.

The door cracked open, and Molly peeked in. "Mom? Are you guys okay? It's already ten o'clock. You're still sleeping?"

"We're okay," Andri said, rubbing her eyes. "We'll be up in a minute."

"Grandma already ate?"

"Yeah," Molly nodded. "I fed the kids, and David and I had some breakfast too."

"Okay. Thanks, honey. We'll be up soon."

Molly gave a quick smile and closed the door gently behind her.

Drew opened his eyes. The first thing he noticed was how sore his legs were.

As yesterday came rushing back, he muttered, "You know, if it hadn't been for Tanya and Leanne, David wouldn't be alive right now."

"God, don't remind me," Andri said, her voice carrying both heartache and relief. She threw the covers back and sat up. "Come on, let's get up. I need to hold and kiss my boy."

Drew let out a dry chuckle. "Because you didn't do enough of that yesterday?"

She smiled, undeterred. "Kissing and holding my children never gets old." Then she leaned in close, eyes sparkling as she added, "Same goes for my handsome man. But... that's for another time."

Drew shook his head, smiling as she walked away.

At the dining room table, Drew sipped his coffee, quietly watching Andri in the living room. She was fussing over David, who looked more amused than bothered as he let her smother him with attention. Drew smiled to himself. He loved Andri deeply, but there was something special about watching her love others; she was all in, no holding back.

His thoughts were interrupted when Lanix walked in and dropped into a chair across from him, holding a glass of orange juice.

"What's up, Lanix?" Drew asked.

Lanix hesitated, then leaned forward. "I overheard some things... about what happened yesterday. Molly and Shannon were talking, but every time they saw me, they'd either go quiet or change the subject. And when I asked, they just said, 'It's nothing to worry about.'" He looked down, then back up, his voice tight. "It's not fair, Drew. I'm part of this family too. I told you before; I want to help protect everyone."

Drew studied him for a moment. The kid looked serious. Hurt, even. And determined.

He thought of Boomer. If anyone could help shape Lanix into someone who could truly hold his own, it was him.

"Lanix," Drew said, setting his cup down, "are you really serious about this? About learning the skills to protect your family? Because this won't be easy. We're talking hard physical training, discipline, mental focus. No quitting. No attitude."

Lanix's eyes widened, not in fear, but in excitement. "Yes. I want that. I really do."

Drew gave a slow nod. "All right. I'll see what I can arrange. But if I manage to set this up... there's no backing out. You follow through."

"There won't be. I promise."

"Good. But I still need to talk to your mother first."

Lanix nodded, gripping his glass a little tighter, a flicker of hope lighting up behind his eyes.

After Lanix left the room, Drew leaned back in his chair and rubbed his chin, still thinking. The kid wasn't just asking to be included; he was asking to be trusted. And maybe he'd earned that.

From the living room, he could still hear Andri talking softly to David, her voice, equal parts nurturing and fuss. David's laugh, weak but genuine, floated into the dining room. It was the best sound Drew had heard in days.

He stood up, coffee in hand, and walked to the edge of the room, leaning against the doorway. Andri looked up, her eyes immediately locking with his. There was that silent communication they'd always had. It was born of years, pain, love, and everything in between.

"I need to talk to you," Drew said gently.

Andri gave David's arm one last squeeze and stood, walking over to him. "Everything okay?"

"Yeah," he said. "It's about Lanix."

She raised an eyebrow, already curious. "What about him?"

"He wants to be trained. Real training. Not just weekend drills with me or Josh. I mean serious stuff: discipline, survival, combat, the works. And I think he's ready."

Andri looked toward the hallway where Lanix had gone, then back at Drew. "You're serious?"

"So is he," Drew said. "He's not a little kid anymore. He wants to protect his family, Andri. I think he feels left out, and he's tired of sitting on the sidelines while the rest of us risk everything."

Her expression softened, but concern crept in. "What kind of training are we talking about?"

"I know someone," Drew said. "A friend of Boomer's. Off-grid. The best there is. If he agrees to take Lanix on, it won't be easy. But it'll change him. Maybe even save him."

Andri nodded slowly, torn between motherly instinct and the hard truth that their lives weren't safe enough to shield anyone anymore.

"Let me think about it," she said. "But thank you for taking him seriously."

"I understand," Drew said gently. "I get that you want to think about it, and why you're concerned. He's your baby, your youngest. Of course you're protective." He reached for her hand. "But, Andri... your family isn't the average kind. There's a lot more coming for all of us.

Lanix is going to need this, whether he ends up using it or not. And if I'm being honest... I have a feeling he will."

Andri nodded, eyes misting with emotion but steady with resolve. "You're right, Drew," she said softly. "I have the same feeling. We have to do what we've got to do."

Drew stepped out onto the back porch, the screen door creaking shut behind him. The late morning sun had burned off most of the clouds, but the wind still carried the storm's chill. He pulled his phone from his pocket and scrolled through his contacts until he found Boomer's number.

He hit call.

Two rings.

"Boomer," came the gruff voice on the other end.

"Hey, it's Drew."

"Drew. You good?"

"Getting there," Drew said, glancing out at the trees swaying gently in the breeze. "It's been a hell of a couple days."

"I heard. Lockjaw filled me in on the storm. Said the place got torn up pretty bad."

"Yeah. And there's more coming; not weather, worse."

There was a short pause on the line. Then Boomer said, "Talk to me."

Drew took a breath. "It's about Lanix. He's ready. He wants in. Not just messing around on the weekends or doing drills with me. He wants real training: discipline, survival, combat, the whole thing."

Boomer gave a low whistle. "The kid... said that?"

"He didn't just say it. He meant it. He's tired of being kept out of the loop. And honestly, I don't blame him."

Boomer went quiet for a beat. Then, "You sure he's ready for the real thing?"

"I told him there's no quitting. No room for ego or half-assed effort. He said he's all in."

"Well," Boomer said, "I know a guy who could get him there. But this ain't lightweight stuff, Drew. This guy doesn't teach classes. He transforms people. He'll push Lanix harder than either of us ever could."

"That who I think it is?"

"Yeah. Ghost."

Drew nodded to himself. "Thought so."

"He doesn't do this kind of thing often," Boomer added. "Last time was a teenager from North Dakota who wanted to join the Rangers. That kid came out a completely different person. Ghost doesn't just train the body. He rewires the whole mindset."

Drew's voice lowered. "You think he'll take Lanix on?"

"He owes me," Boomer said. "But I'm not cashing that in unless you're serious."

"I am. And so is Lanix. I already talked to Andri. She agrees."

Boomer let out a slow exhale. "All right. I'll reach out. Just know this: once Ghost accepts, there's no halfway. If Lanix walks onto that property, he walks off changed. One way or another."

"That's exactly what I'm counting on."

Boomer chuckled softly. "You always did know when to play your cards. I'll be in touch."

Drew ended the call and stood in the silence a moment longer, phone still in hand, heart steady. He had a feeling the real storm hadn't even started yet.

Later that afternoon, Drew stood in the hallway just outside Lanix's room. The door was slightly open, and he could hear soft music playing from a speaker. He knocked once.

"Lanix," he called. "Got a minute?"

Lanix looked up from his desk and nodded. "Yeah, come in."

Drew stepped inside, shutting the door behind him. He stayed standing, arms crossed, his face more serious than before.

"I need to talk to you one more time. No jokes. No hype. Just the truth."

Lanix straightened in his chair.

"I spoke to Boomer," Drew said. "There's a man who might take you on; might train you. But this isn't just learning how to throw a punch or handle a weapon. This man will break you down and rebuild you. You walk onto his land, you don't come back the same. There's no 'I'm tired,' no 'I changed my mind,' no calling it off halfway through."

Lanix's throat tightened, but he didn't look away.

Drew stepped closer, locking eyes with him. "You said you wanted to protect your family. This is your shot to back that up. But I need your word. Once this starts, you finish it. You come out the person you told me you wanted to be."

Lanix took a breath, heart pounding. Then he stood up slowly, facing Drew.

"You have my word," he said. "I won't quit."

Drew held his gaze for a long second, then gave a slow, firm nod. "All right. I'll make the call."

As Drew left the room, Lanix stood still, watching the door ease shut behind him. His heart was beating harder now, a steady drum of adrenaline and anticipation.

This is it, he thought.

He looked around his room: the desk, the shelves, the half-finished video game still paused on his screen. All of it suddenly felt... smaller.

My life's about to change. No more just being the kid in the background. No more wasting time in front of screens.

I'm going to become what I always dreamed of. What I was meant to be.

He didn't know exactly what lay ahead, but for the first time, he didn't feel afraid.

He felt ready.

Andri was on the phone when Drew came upstairs from the basement. He slowed his steps as he reached the top, immediately noticing the look on her face, surprised, maybe even a little concerned.

He moved closer, trying to hear.

The house was unusually quiet. David and the girls were in the living room, the TV still on, but David had lowered the volume. All of them were glancing toward the kitchen, listening. No one said a word.

Andri's voice was hushed but clear.

"Really? Already? You're here?"

She paused, then added, "I didn't know you were coming... Okay, um, we'll see you in a few."

A small pause. "All right, brother. Is everything okay? Joe?"

She listened, her expression unreadable. "Okay, well... I guess we'll hear what you've got to say when you get here."

She ended the call and looked around the room.

"That was Joe," she said. "And Kelly, Joe's wife.

They're in Nebraska. They just flew in, and now they're on their way here."

Drew raised an eyebrow. "Here? Today?"

"They want to talk to the family," Andri said. "Joe asked if Leanne and Josh could come over too." She looked down for a second, then back at Drew. "I don't know what's going on." Andri picked up her phone and dialed Leanne.

As soon as she answered, Andri got straight to the point.

"Joe's on his way over. He asked if you could come down. Said he needs to talk to all of us."

Leanne's voice came through the speaker, thoughtful. "I wonder what he has to say. I wonder what's going on."

"I don't know," Andri admitted. "He didn't say much. I just hope nobody's sick..."

Then she caught herself and shook her head. "No, let's not jump to that. We'll hear what he has to say when he gets here. No use worrying until we know."

"Okay," Leanne replied. "Should I bring Josh and Shannon too? All of us?"

"Yeah," Andri said. "All of you."

"All right. We're on our way."

Andri hung up the call and slipped the phone into her pocket.

She turned and walked down the hallway into Nora's room, where the older woman was just waking up from her nap. Sunlight slanted in through the curtains as Andri helped her sit up, brushing her hair gently and guiding her to the living room.

Once Nora was settled into the rocking chair, Andri knelt beside her.

"Mom, Joe's coming over," she said softly. "He wants to say hello to all of us."

Nora's eyes lit up with recognition and joy. She clapped her hands and smiled wide. "Oh, how nice. That's wonderful."

Andri smiled back, though a flicker of curiosity still lingered in her chest.

Everyone shuffled into the great room, Andri and Drew taking the small loveseat, Nora settling into her rocking chair, the others finding space across the sectional couch and on scattered chairs. Lanix dropped cross-legged onto the floor beside Molly, already sensing something big was about to unfold.

Just as Joe stepped to the front of the room, Kelly turned toward the TV stand and grabbed the remote. "Hold on," she said. "We've got one more joining us."

She clicked the remote, and the big screen on the wall flickered to life. A moment later, the familiar ding of a Zoom connection sounded.

Then Michael's face appeared, clear, smiling, and a little pixelated. "Hey!" he said with a wave. "I'm here. Sorry for the time delay. I'm still in Scotland."

"Michael!" Andri beamed. "We were just about to start."

"Joe gave me the heads up this morning. Sounds like we've got something serious to talk about."

Joe nodded toward the screen. "Glad you could make it, brother."

Michael leaned in, his tone light but curious. "So, what's going on?"

Joe exhaled and glanced around the room again. Everyone was here. Everyone was watching. The air was heavy with waiting.

"I was in Sedona yesterday," he began, his voice steady but tinged with something heavier. "With Tanya."

A wave of surprised murmurs passed through the room.

"She asked me to come," he continued. "This wasn't just a check-in. She had something to show me, something to tell me. And it's about all of us."

He paused, eyes scanning his family, his voice calm, but his presence charged with urgency.

And then, with everyone watching, Michael from thousands of miles away, Nora from her rocker, and Lanix from the floor, Joe began to tell the story.

When Joe finished speaking, the room fell silent.

Not an awkward silence, but the kind that fills a space when everyone's trying to process the same impossible truth. A weight hung in the air, settling into the furniture, into their bones.

Eyes shifted from one person to another. Nobody quite knew what to say first.

Then Leanne broke the quiet with a sudden laugh, half disbelief, half nerves. "Wait. Are you serious? We're... moving to Arizona?"

All eyes turned to her.

"I've never even been to Arizona," she said, still chuckling. "I don't want to move to a desert. I like my trees. I like not sweating through my clothes before breakfast."

Josh smirked. "You already sweat through your clothes if you even look at a sunny window."

"Shut up," Leanne shot back, though her grin took the sting out of it.

Andri smiled faintly, but her voice was steady when she spoke. "It's not about where we want to live anymore. It's about where we're supposed to be."

Josh sat back, arms crossed, his expression thoughtful. "Tanya always said Sedona was special. If she's building something there, and we're part of it... we don't really have a choice, do we?"

Joe looked around the room again. "No one's forcing anyone. But Tanya made it clear. Mystic Crossroads can't survive without us. And if we want to keep the portals protected, keep our people safe, we have to be there. Together."

Lanix sat up straighter on the floor. "So... when do we go?"

Joe gave a small smile. "Soon. The place is already being built. Tanya's crew is fast. She left everything in order. It's happening."

The room fell quiet again, but this time it wasn't filled with confusion. It was filled with a shift, an invisible, silent acceptance.

The family didn't have all the answers yet, but they knew the road ahead was already being laid out for them.

David stood up and stretched with a groan. "Well," he said dryly, "I guess we better start packing."

He looked around the room. "Let me know which houses you want me to list. Since I'm the guy in real estate, I'll get them on the market by tomorrow morning."

He paused, then added with a smirk, "Looks like I'm in charge of relocating the chosen ones."

The room, heavy a moment ago, lifted with laughter.

Chapter 9

The New Beginning

All the homes had been sold, and the families had officially moved on to Sedona. It had been a week since they'd settled into their new houses, tucked close together like a modern-day village, one built on faith, family, and something far deeper than any of them could explain.

They still couldn't quite believe how beautiful it all was.

Red rocks surrounded them like ancient guardians, and the light seemed different here, warmer, more alive. There was peace in the air, yet it pulsed with unseen energy, as if the land itself were waiting for something. The moon seemed to sense it too, casting a bright, protective ray that fell directly upon the Mystic Crossroads shop, as though guarding it from the darkness beyond.

They were grateful to have homes circling one another like a private compound, a place to raise their children, train, heal, and prepare. The new Mystic Crossroads store stood ready at the center of it all, an elegant, old-world building. There was space inside for herbs, books, mirrors, and things they hadn't even discovered yet.

The sealed envelope still sat untouched in the display cabinet, right at the heart of the store. No one had dared open it. Not yet. Joe had insisted they wait. "Let's settle in first," he told them. "Then we'll face what comes next."

But now it was time for the next step.

Joe had gathered everyone and said, "Before we open that envelope, there's one thing we have to do. Tanya asked that we all come see her at her farmhouse in Superior. She wants to see us, all of us, together."

So plans were made, bags packed, and the family prepared to travel southeast to Tanya's farmhouse one last time.

Two weeks earlier, before they left their old town, the family had come together for a dinner in Lanix's honor. It was a night filled with laughter, tears, and the weight of goodbyes. Lanix had set off for summer training with Ghost, his journey just beginning. Boomer had pulled Drew aside that night, clapped him on the back, and said, "I'll look after him, brother. He'll come back strong. You have my word." That same dinner was also for Molly. She was heading off to the military, and though the pride in the room ran deep, the ache of her absence was already setting in.

Now, as the sun rose over Sedona and cast long golden streaks across their new beginning, the remaining family members packed up their vehicles and prepared for the drive to Superior.

None of them knew exactly why Tanya had asked them to come, but when Tanya asked, they listened.

And whatever she had to say, they were ready to hear it.

The drive to Superior stretched out under a cloudless blue sky, the desert landscape shifting around them as red cliffs gave way to flatter terrain, dotted with cacti, mesquite, and rugged rock. The family traveled in a loose caravan, three vehicles, one behind the other, winding their way through Arizona's long desert roads. The occasional radio crackle or hand wave through a window kept the line connected. As they neared the outskirts of Superior, the narrow roads began to open into a wide, dusty clearing. Just beyond it stood Tanya's farmhouse.

It was larger than most had pictured, more sprawling than grand, with weathered white siding, a wraparound porch shaded by creaking beams, and a view that stretched toward the mountains. Wildflowers grew around the property in soft bursts of yellow and purple, stubbornly blooming against the dry earth.

On the porch, Tanya stood waiting, her figure framed by the wooden posts and filtered sunlight. She waved when she saw them coming, a soft smile on her face that carried both joy and something unreadable.

The vehicles pulled in one by one, crunching over gravel, engines cutting as doors swung open. Everyone stepped out, stretching limbs from the long ride and shaking off the road dust.

Leanne took Nora's hand gently and helped her out of the backseat. "Watch your step, Mom," she said, guiding her carefully along the walkway.

Tanya descended the porch steps to greet them. One by one, she embraced them: Joe, Kelly, Andri, Josh, Shannon, David, and Drew. Her hugs were strong but unhurried, her eyes locking with each of theirs as if memorizing every face. Kelly handed her a bouquet of fresh flowers, which Tanya accepted with a soft, grateful nod.

An extra vehicle pulled in just behind the last of the caravan, sending up a gentle swirl of dust. From it stepped Michael, freshly arrived from Scotland, and Skye, Joe and Kelly's daughter, who had flown in earlier that day from visiting a friend in San Diego. They had met up at Phoenix Sky Harbor Airport, where Michael had landed just an hour before her. He'd waited for her in the terminal, and together they'd rented a car and made the drive east to catch up with the family.

Tanya's eyes lit up as she saw them approaching, arms full of small overnight bags and light jackets. She wrapped Michael in a long, silent hug, then did the same with Skye. She'd never met them, but they were family just the same.

Once bags had been brought inside and shoes kicked off by the door, Tanya motioned them all toward the heart of the home, a wide, sunlit great room that seemed to hum with quiet energy.

"Come on in," she said. "We've got some catching up to do."

The great room was full, but somehow quiet, comfortably so. Pillows had been passed around. Lemonade, coffee, and cold drinks were in everyone's hands. Tanya had invited them all in to sit, not for any big announcement yet, just to catch up. The couches and chairs were loosely arranged in a circle, with Nora in a special seat by the wide window, Skye beside her, gently holding her hand.

Tanya looked from face to face, listening as everyone talked about the move to Sedona. There were jokes about learning new street names, surprise at how quickly Anio's crew had finished the houses, and gratitude for finally being together again. She smiled as they shared their little stories, Skye finding a scorpion in her new bathroom, Shannon talking about the energy of the red rocks, Andri describing how Nora lit up every morning with her tea by the porch.

But the tone shifted slightly when David raised his hand.

"There's something I need to bring up," he said. "We brought someone with us. His name's Todd."

He stood and motioned toward the hallway. Moments later, Todd stepped hesitantly into the room.

"This is him," David continued. "We're trying to get him home, but we've got a problem."

He explained everything: how Todd came from the Red World, how they'd discovered him, the events that followed, and the complications now sitting squarely in their laps.

The room grew still. Tanya folded her hands together, her eyes locked on Todd for a long moment before she finally spoke.

"He can't go back to the Red World," she said calmly. "The portal meant for that world was destroyed in the tornado. It was always fragile... and Anio didn't want a doorway to the Red World left open."

David frowned. "So there's no way to rebuild it?"

"Even if there were," Tanya said gently, "what then? He's twenty-five. He's supposed to be fifty-five. How do you explain that? How do you place him in a life that's not waiting for him anymore?"

That sank in for a moment.

Joe leaned forward. "What about the portals in Sedona? Is there another option there?"

Tanya nodded thoughtfully. "That could be the answer. But you'll have to read everything inside the sealed envelope first: every rule, every step. Nothing can be rushed or skipped. If it's done right, you might find something that helps."

Someone asked, "Could we send him to a different world that's just like this one?"

Leanne raised a skeptical eyebrow. "Even if we did, he'd still be in the same situation. No ID. No birth certificate. And what if there's already a Todd Edmonds in that world? Then what?"

Heads nodded around the room. She was right.

David spoke again, slower this time. "What if... we don't bring him back to the present? What if we send him into this world's past? Somewhere he could still live under blue skies. Somewhere he'd belong."

Everyone turned toward him.

"What do you mean?" Shannon asked.

"In the past," David said, "there's no paperwork. No ID requirements. No databases. All he'd need is a name and a story. He could say he lost everything in a fire. It happened all the time. At least in the Red Earth it did. He could survive. Start over."

Andri nodded slowly. "But he'd have to go way back. Far enough that nobody would question it."

"Yeah," Joe added. "Maybe the early 1900s. Or even the late 1800s."

Michael raised an eyebrow, clearly unimpressed. "Oh, sure, just hop in a time portal and become a cowboy. Makes total sense."

Todd's eyes widened. "Are you guys serious right now?"

All eyes turned to him.

"Yes," David said. "We're not kidding."

Josh leaned forward, a crooked grin tugging at the corner of his mouth. "No, I don't think we need to send him that far back. Come on. I think the 1950s, maybe early '60s, they probably accepted losers without paperwork. I'm sure they did."

He looked over at Todd with mock helpfulness. "That would be a better fit, right?"

Drew shot him a look. "Now, come on. There's no need to call him a loser. He did save David from the building. Give the guy some credit."

Josh shrugged. "Yeah, well, you didn't have the experience I had with him."

Tanya lifted a hand calmly. "It's true. He could go back and live in the 1950s or early '60s. Honestly, post-war-1940s would work better. Less oversight, more flexibility."

Todd threw his hands up, exasperated. "I can't believe this."

And then, quietly but firmly, Michael spoke up.

"Listen, Todd, or whoever you are. I don't know you, and frankly, I don't believe a word of this whole story. I don't know what happened to my family since I've been gone, but let's just pretend it's all true. Let's say you are from another world and all this actually happened."

He stood, crossing his arms, eyes fixed on Todd.

"You're acting like this is some kind of punishment. Meanwhile, the people in this room, people I love, are trying to help you start over. They're willing to teach you how to survive in a new time, help you adapt, maybe even give you a decent life. And instead of gratitude, you're throwing a fit."

Michael's voice dropped just slightly. "From what I hear, your plans for my nephews were just so heartwarming," he said with sarcasm. "The only reason you're even standing here, getting this little heart-to-heart, is because you dragged my nephew out of that building. Otherwise? You'd be long gone."

Silence fell over the room. Todd's jaw clenched, but he didn't say anything.

Everyone turned to Todd.

His face reddened, not with anger this time, but something quieter. Shame. Maybe even guilt.

He looked around the room, and for the first time, he truly seemed to grasp the weight of the situation.

He was caught between worlds, literally, and the window to return home had been destroyed. The Red World was no longer an option. And here, in this modern world, he couldn't even rent a room without paperwork, let alone live a life.

For a long moment, he said nothing. Then he nodded slowly, eyes lowered in thought.

"I guess... post war-1940s could work," he said. "I could learn to live in that time. I could rebuild. I know how to start things from scratch. Maybe even open a business. Hell, maybe I could fall in love. Have a family. Be... someone."

He looked up, a strange steadiness in his voice now. "I'm a man. I can do this."

He rose to his feet and met everyone's eyes in turn.

"1946... 1947..." He paused, then nodded with finality.

"1947 it is."

Tanya stood up, her long skirt swaying gently as she moved to the center of the room.

"Good," she said, her voice steady. "1947 it is."

She turned toward Drew and Josh. "I need you two to drive into town. There's a coin and collectible shop on Main Street. Buy as many coins and bills as you can find that date before 1947. Paper money too. As much as they'll sell you."

Josh blinked. "Uh... won't that be expensive?"

Tanya reached into a side table drawer and handed him a thick envelope, already sealed and ready.

"Don't worry about it," she said. "Just do it."

Drew eyed the envelope, then glanced at the others. "How did you—?"

He stopped himself and sighed. "Never mind. She's Tanya."

The room chuckled.

Tanya then looked over to where Skye sat on the floor. "Skye, can you help Todd? Teach him how to blend in. How to speak, how to move, what to wear. He needs to understand how to survive in 1947."

Skye perked up, already opening her laptop. "On it. We'll go over slang, customs, tech (well, lack of it), and the basics. We'll make him a proper time traveler."

Todd looked around the room, still slightly overwhelmed, but now wearing the faintest trace of a grin. For the first time, he felt something like direction.

The room began to stir with quiet motion, people rising, making plans, preparing. The mood had shifted. The unknown was still ahead, but now, so was a plan.

And Tanya, as always, had known exactly what needed to be done.

———◆———

Later that evening, as the sun dipped low behind the hills of Superior, the energy in Tanya's farmhouse shifted. The earlier conversations had given way to action.

Todd stood in the great room, his hands loosely at his sides, heart pounding in his chest. He had made his decision: 1947 Los Angeles. The future, for him, now lived in the past.

Josh and Drew returned from town with two small bags, coins, bills, and silver pieces dating from the 1930s and '40s, still warm from their hands. Todd was handed the satchel, eyes widening at the weight of it.

"This should get you started," Drew said. "Land, livestock... a second chance."

Tanya stood beside Leanne, holding the mirror with both hands. "It's time," she said quietly. "But Leanne, I want you to do it."

"Me?" Leanne's eyes widened.

Tanya nodded. "It's your role now. I'll guide you."

Skye stepped forward, holding out a small manila envelope. "Everything you need to know about 1947 is in here: language, customs, slang, prices... even how to act like you're used to rotary phones and... to be sure to tip your milkman. You'll be okay."

Todd looked at the envelope, then at Skye and smiled. "Thank you."

Joe added with a smirk, "Good thing you're from the Red Earth. Otherwise, you'd be rich just betting on game scores and world events. But since you don't know shit about it... you can't cheat."

As he took it, the mirror began to shimmer faintly in Tanya's hands. Leanne reached out, placing one hand gently on the glass as Tanya whispered a quiet set of instructions only she could hear.

The mirror pulsed.

Suddenly, Michael stepped back, eyebrows raised, jaw slack. "Are you seeing this?" he muttered. "Are those... new clothes?"

Todd glanced down just as his worn jeans and T-shirt shimmered and shifted, replaced by neatly pressed high-waisted slacks, a button-up shirt, suspenders, and polished shoes. A simple wool coat rested over one arm, and a well-worn hat appeared tucked into his belt.

He looked like he had walked straight out of another time.

"No, Uncle Michael, not new clothes," Paula breathed, eyes wide. "Old ones."

Todd turned to face them all one last time. His eyes scanned the room: David, who had fought for him to stay alive; Josh, who hadn't trusted him for good reason; Andri, who had offered calm without question; Drew, who had shown respect; and Skye, who had made sure he'd be ready.

Before saying anything else, he took a breath and cleared his throat.

"I need to say something," he began, quieter now. "To all of you, but especially Josh and David."

The room stilled.

"I came back into your lives with... the wrong intentions. I was angry. Stupid. I let my ego take over, and I let that justify what I was planning to do to you both, along with Andrea. I can't take that back, and I'll carry it with me. But I want you to know. I'm sorry. Truly. You didn't owe me kindness, but you gave it anyway. And I don't take that for granted."

David offered a look of quiet acknowledgment, and Josh gave him the smallest nod. It was enough.

Then Todd held up the bag of money. "I'm gonna buy land," he said. "Outskirts of the city. I know how to raise animals. Maybe I'll start something real. A business, a life. I'm only twenty-five. I've got time."

He smiled faintly. "Might even fall in love."

Andri's eyes misted.

Leanne's too.

"Thank you," Todd added. "For giving me a future I wasn't supposed to have."

He paused, eyes sweeping over the family one last time.

"I hope you all remember me," he said softly. "As the man who lived in three worlds."

Then, without hesitation, he turned to the mirror. Leanne placed her finger flat against the glass and whispered the date. The shimmer thickened, swirled, and then... he was gone.

Only silence remained.

Chapter 10

The wind over Superior was different that morning, soft, fragrant, and strangely still, as if the land itself were listening.

After breakfast, Skye, Paula, and the twins, Daphne and Delilah, sat in the upstairs loft, tapping quietly on their laptops.

Outside on the back porch, David, Leanne, Kelly, Josh, and Shannon sipped coffee, their voices low and reflective.

Inside the great room, Michael, Joe, and Drew sat with Nora and Andri. The quiet hum of the house seemed to echo with something unspoken.

"Michael, are you doing okay?" Andri asked gently.

Michael looked over at her, his expression distant. "I can't process this... and I don't want to talk about it right now."

Andri gave a concerned nod but didn't press him.

Just then, Tanya entered the room with her usual calm presence. She looked directly at Michael.

"If your skepticism is still that strong," she said, "I suggest you sit out the next family meeting." She paused, then added, "But I don't recommend it. This is your family, Michael. And it's time to come to terms with that."

She turned to Andri. "Andri, please call the rest of the family. That next meeting is now."

Tanya took her seat in her armchair, facing the couches. Nora stood quietly, then walked over and sat in the second armchair beside her. The two women sat side by side, calm and regal, facing the room like a pair of elders holding court.

As the rest of the family filtered in, they glanced at one another, curious and a little unsettled.

Why is Nora sitting beside Tanya like that?

What's going on?

Something was about to happen. They could all feel it.

Before the meeting began, Michael sat quietly, Tanya's words still echoing in his head. He didn't like being spoken to so directly, especially not in front of everyone. But deep down, he knew she was right.

He rubbed the bridge of his nose, his mind spinning. *You're a quantum physicist, for God's sake.* A man of equations, probabilities, and theories that danced just on the edge of what most people considered real. He'd devoted his life to understanding the invisible fabric of the universe, particles that appeared and disappeared, realities that overlapped, probabilities that changed depending on who was watching.

And yet, watching a man's clothes morph before his eyes... watching someone vanish through a mirror... That wasn't science.

Or was it?

He exhaled slowly and looked around the room. He had always known, deep down, that his family wasn't like other families. He'd seen things as a kid, overheard whispers, felt strange shifts in the air that no one could explain. But he'd buried it all under degrees and logic. Under lab coats and published papers. He didn't want to be part of this. He didn't want to remember.

But he did remember.

And that scared him more than he liked to admit.

Michael's eyes flicked over to Tanya, seated in that oversized armchair like some ancient keeper of forgotten truths. She hadn't flinched when addressing him, hadn't softened her tone. She didn't treat him like a scientist. She treated him like a man who needed to show up for his family.

He still didn't understand any of this, not really. And he sure as hell didn't believe in "magic mirrors" or portals to other worlds. But he also hadn't walked out of the room.

So he stayed. Because something told him, whether he liked it or not, that anything could happen next.

And it probably would.

Everyone was seated in the great room now, nestled in armchairs, sharing couches, perched at the edges of coffee tables and windowsills. The sun had started to dip low, casting a warm golden hue through the farmhouse windows. The chatter had quieted. Even the children upstairs had gone still.

Tanya stood near the fireplace, her posture regal yet softened by the weight of what she was about to say. Nora sat beside her, hands folded gently in her lap, her eyes shining with quiet awareness.

Tanya took a breath, then looked around the room with a calm, unwavering gaze.

"I've called you all here because I have something important to share," she began. "Anio told me a month ago that when the time came, I would not be sent to another town, another store, or another role to manage. My transition wouldn't be earthly. My life... would be moving on."

There was silence. A few confused glances. Then, a collective sharp inhale, a ripple of reaction as her words registered.

"What?" someone whispered. Another voice said softly, "No..."

Tanya held up a hand, steady and serene. "Please, let me finish."

She glanced toward Shannon, and her eyes softened. "Before I go, I want to leave something behind, something important. Shannon..." she said, and her voice caught just slightly, "You've worked beside me at Mystic Crossroads. You've been like a daughter to me. This envelope," she said, holding out a thick parchment sealed with an unfamiliar symbol, "belongs to you."

Shannon's chin trembled as she stood up, her hands clasped over her mouth. "No... no, not like this," she said, tears filling her eyes.

"There's more," Tanya said gently, still holding the envelope.

And then everything shifted.

From the far side of the room, where the sunlight had dimmed, a shimmer of gold began to ripple in the air. A soft, resonant hum seemed to vibrate from the walls themselves. The shimmer widened, unfolding like the petals of an invisible flower, and within it came a slow cascade of glowing orbs, no larger than dragonflies, but with radiant, winged light trailing behind them.

They moved with grace and intention, spiraling and dancing in the space between Tanya and the family, their presence electrifying and gentle all at once.

Some of the women in the room covered their hearts with their hands, eyes brimming with tears. The energy wasn't frightening. It was beautiful. Pure. Sacred.

Even the men, speechless, stared wide-eyed at the spectacle unfolding. Leanne clutched David's arm. Josh took a cautious step forward. Michael... said nothing.

The lights moved in patterns, spiraling, weaving, merging, until they coalesced into a single being. A luminous, soft outline of a figure stood in the space now glowing with warmth and silence.

Anio had arrived.

The shimmer of Anio's presence pulsed softly in the room, a heartbeat of light that seemed to cradle the moment in something greater.

Tanya turned from the radiant figure and looked back at Shannon. Her voice was steady. "Open the envelope, sweetheart."

Shannon shook her head, tears already slipping down her cheeks. "No," she whispered, her voice cracking. "No, you're not going anywhere."

Josh quietly rose and stepped beside her, placing both hands on her trembling shoulders. He leaned close, whispering something just for her, steadying her.

"Please," Tanya said again, more gently now. "Open it."

With trembling fingers, Shannon broke the seal. Inside were a small set of silver keys, a folded deed, and a safe deposit box key tucked into a worn envelope. She stared down at the items in disbelief, her breath catching. As the realization hit her... she began to cry, not from joy, not entirely from sorrow, but from the overwhelming truth of what it meant.

She sank into Josh, who caught her in his arms, holding her as her body shook.

Tanya stepped forward, her gaze full of love. "I wanted you to have it," she said softly. "This home. Everything I built. It's time for you to live a little now, Shannon. Not to serve, just to live. To enjoy. To breathe."

Shannon couldn't speak. She just clung to Josh, one hand still gripping the keys.

The family remained silent, the weight of the moment pressing down like a reverent hush. The energy from Anio's presence continued to pulse gently, wrapping the room in something not entirely explainable, but deeply understood.

One by one, they approached her: Andri, Leanne, Josh, David, even Joe. Each took Tanya into their arms, not rushing, not holding back. Their embraces were full and long, the kind reserved for those rare, sacred goodbyes. Words came in quiet fragments. "Thank you," "I love you," "I'm glad we got this moment."

Josh said it best. "Most people don't get a chance to say goodbye like this. I'm grateful we do."

The rest of the family nodded through their tears. Some hugged her tightly, others simply reached out to touch her shoulder or hand, not trusting their voices. Even in their sorrow, a soft peace wrapped around them. The kind that says this ending... wasn't really the end.

Then Nora stood.

Tanya smiled wide, her arms already outstretched. They embraced like two souls who had walked a thousand lifetimes together.

"Sister," Tanya whispered. "Sister in spirit."

Nora gave a quiet nod, wiping at her eyes. "It's time," she said softly.

The air shimmered.

Anio lifted his arms, those radiant arms aglow with golden light, pulsing and flowing like sunlight on water. Every movement sent gentle waves of light through the space, like music only the soul could hear.

Tanya turned to the family one last time.

Her eyes sparkled with joy, not fear, not sorrow. Just peace.

And then she stepped into him.

In that instant, her body dissolved into a flurry of luminous particles, like tiny winged stars, and they danced, shimmering, before merging into Anio's light. The room filled with warmth, with beauty so overwhelming that several in the room gasped, others smiled through their tears. Someone whispered, "She's free."

Then, as the light settled, a silhouette formed beside Anio. It was her.

Tanya, but not as she had been.

She was radiant, youthful, smiling. She looked around at the family, her voice not heard but felt, spoken directly to the heart.

"It is wonderful. Don't be sad for me."

They watched in stillness, not sure whether to cry or to laugh. The beauty of it confused their grief, turned it into something softer.

But as Tanya and Anio remained there, not fading, just standing, watching, the family began to wonder.

Why are they still here?

What was still unfinished?

And in the hush that followed, no one dared to speak. Only the sense that something more was coming... lingered in the air.

And then Nora spoke.

Her voice, clear, strong, and startlingly lucid, cut through the silence like the sudden lifting of fog.

Everyone turned.

Gone was the distant look in her eyes, the gentle confusion that had settled over her in recent years. She stood tall, grounded in her presence, her gaze steady and knowing.

"Anio is still here," she said softly, "because I'm going too."

Gasps rippled through the room.

"I'm going with Anio and Tanya," she said softly. "It's my time, too. That's why we were all called here."

A strangled sound escaped Andri's throat as her knees gave out beneath her.

"No, Mom... no. Please," she sobbed, crawling forward like a child reaching for safety.

Drew rushed to her side, lifting her gently from the floor, wrapping her in his arms as she trembled.

Michael stepped closer, stunned. "Mom... you can't just leave," he whispered, as if saying it any louder might make it more real.

Across the room, Joe and Leanne clung to each other, silent and shaking.

The grandchildren were crying, some quietly, others unable to hold back the heartbreak.

Sobs and gasps filled the air, each one echoing the ache none of them were ready to face.

Nora lowered herself to meet her daughter and cupped her face with hands that no longer trembled. "Mija," she said gently, "I've lived my life. I've loved my life and my children. But these last few years... that wasn't living. I've been trapped in a mind that couldn't hold the memories I cherished most."

She kissed Andri's forehead. "But now... now I am whole again. I can go forward into something beautiful. I won't be lost anymore."

The room held its breath. No one moved.

Nora turned, her hands relaxed at her sides, and took a step toward the radiant light where Anio and Tanya still stood. The same shimmer enveloped her, recognizing her readiness.

Because Nora knew it had to be now. If they lined up to hug her, one by one, sobbing and holding on, she wouldn't be able to go. And she knew that. It was better this way.

She paused just before crossing the threshold and looked back once more, her eyes full of peace.

"I'll be watching," she whispered.

The two women stood beside him, smiling, radiant. Tanya's voice came through one last time, soft and loving: "It was wonderful. Don't be sad for us."

They lingered a moment longer, then faded together, leaving behind warmth, peace, and a silence filled with awe.

They were free.

Next in the Series: *LEANNE*